£2.45

THE DIVIDING LINE

The scene is Agadir after the earthquake of 1960. In the after-math of horror and confusion Simon Perry, a footloose failure, finds himself alone and friendless in Morocco. While recovering from his injuries in hospital, he accepts the identity of a man he has seen buried alive – along with a new passport, a rich haul of travellers' cheques and a valuable letter of credit from a Swiss bank.

Other works by Robin Maugham

Novels
THE SERVANT
LINE ON GINGER
THE ROUGH AND THE SMOOTH
BEHIND THE MIRROR
THE MAN WITH TWO SHADOWS
NOVEMBER REEF
THE GREEN SHADE
THE SECOND WINDOW
THE LINK
THE WRONG PEOPLE
THE LAST ENCOUNTER
THE BARRIER
THE SIGN
KNOCK ON TEAK
LOVERS IN EXILE

Short stories
THE BLACK TENT AND OTHER STORIES

Travel
COME TO DUST
NOMAD
APPROACH TO PALESTINE
NORTH AFRICAN NOTEBOOK
JOURNEY TO SIWA
THE SLAVES OF TIMBUKTU
THE JOYITA MYSTERY

Biography
SOMERSET AND ALL THE MAUGHAMS

Autobiography
ESCAPE FROM THE SHADOWS
SEARCH FOR NIRVANA

THE
DIVIDING LINE

Robin Maugham

W. H. ALLEN . LONDON
A Howard & Wyndham Company
1979

Photoset, printed and bound in Great Britain by
Redwood Burn Limited, Trowbridge & Esher
for the Publishers, W.H. Allen & Co. Ltd,
44 Hill Street, London W1X 8LB

ISBN 0 491 02314 6

For Andy

Foreword

I was in the Agadir earthquake which took place on 29 February 1960. I had visited Morocco frequently before then, and I have visited it several times since. But all the characters in this novel are imaginary.

Chapter 1

The bar at the Hotel Saada was almost empty that night in February 1960, because a dance was being held in the ballroom downstairs. The band played badly and noisily, and was now attempting a medley from *Gigi*. Simon Perry knew no one in Agadir. He had only arrived at the hotel that afternoon. The bored and sleepy Moroccan barman was slowly polishing some glasses. The smiling genial face of the King, Mohammed V, stared down from between rows of bottles, their different colours reflected in the mirrored shelves. Opposite Simon there was an elegantly dressed, middle-aged man who, like Simon, looked to be in his early forties. Both men were slim and of the same medium height, but while the man opposite Simon looked agreeably content, Simon felt that his own face might disclose frustration and a sense of being defeated by life. His face was tanned, but each morning he saw in the mirror lines of anxiety and fatigue; yet women still seemed to find him attractive. Standing there at the bar, he was suddenly acutely conscious that his suit was creased and worn. He felt lonely and depressed and wondered whether he might go down to the ballroom and try his chances. There must be some woman, lonely and desirable . . . perhaps not, perhaps he would wait. Tomorrow he would be more relaxed, more sure of himself.

At that moment the man turned his head and noticed that Simon was staring at him. Simon smiled without knowing quite why and then found himself buying the stranger a drink.

'Whisky and soda,' the man said, shaking his head in mock despair. 'Terrible din,' he added, pointing to the ballroom below. 'My room is above this bar and I can't sleep . . . so I decided to get up again and come down here for a night-cap.'

'With any luck it will be over by midnight,' Simon replied. He glanced at the bar. For a second he thought the bottles had slid, almost imperceptibly, as if the mirrored shelves had heaved and then settled. The barman noticed his momentary dismay; he shrugged.

'I'm surprised how cool it is,' the stranger said. 'But it seems that after the sun has set, the temperature can be quite low even on the edge of the Sahara.' They began chatting. Neither of them had visited Morocco before; each of them had heard about Agadir and this new hotel on the beach; neither of them had any friends in Morocco. They were both casual, implying they had come here for a short rest, to get away from things, yet they were both wary as if careful to guard a secret.

'My name's Simon Perry,' he said. 'I've retired. I used to run a rubber plantation in Malaya. But I came into an inheritance, so I thought I might as well start enjoying life.'

You're lying again, Simon thought to himself. You'll be telling him next it was great-aunt Millie who died. So what if I did lie? You have to make an impression in this life or else they trample on you.

But the stranger said nothing, he was staring into his glass of whisky. Occasionally a man from the ballroom would drift in for a drink and then return to the dance. Simon waited; he felt uneasy; the air seemed to be weighed down. When the band stopped playing he could hear the sluggish swell of the ocean as it lapped the shore, as if that too was tired.

'I emigrated to Geneva,' the stranger said, 'because of the taxes in England.'

For some reason, perhaps because he was weary and a little drunk, Simon had an urge to speak, to tell this stranger every-thing about himself, to make a confession, but he knew he hadn't the courage. Yet there was something impregnable about this man that he wanted to shatter, he was too suave, too well-heeled.

'I'm an only child,' Simon heard himself saying. 'My parents were killed in the blitz before my regiment was posted to Malaya.' That at least was true, and the orphan touch had always moved women: the man merely nodded and said nothing.

The trouble is, Simon thought, there was so much that was painful in his life that he'd always wanted to suppress the truth and believed only in the fantasy.

'Jungle fighting was pure hell,' he told the stranger. 'Half of the men under my command died of dysentery before we saw the fighting.' A vision of Corporal Perry crouched in the scrub, with his guts coiled in a knot of pain, returned for a second; lowering his eyes he studied the stranger, noticing the well-manicured nails, the tailored cream linen jacket. Escaping taxation, he thought. No lack of funds there.

'What did you do in the war?' Simon asked.

'Medics. In London first, then France and Germany.'

'So you missed out on the Far East? Well, after the war you could make a fortune there, if you were lucky. I stayed on. There was nothing to make me go back to England.'

He had known a few men with private fortunes already, the public school lot, believing in fair play, British Justice – the best in the world. When it came to the crunch there was little of that for him; he had fallen in love with the wife of a planter and that sod wouldn't even give her a divorce. A couple of doubtful deals . . . well, he needed to show them that he could live in style too. All hushed up. Bad for the colony. The British still had to show an example to the natives after all.

'How long are you going to stay here?' the man asked.

'Africa has always intrigued me. Thought I'd travel around. I spent a few weeks in Kenya, but politically it's still too unstable. These states like Morocco that are independent now, what do they feel about foreigners? I mean, could one buy land and start a business?'

Again there was a pause. The man sipped his drink casually; it was almost as if he hadn't heard.

'You're very cagey,' Simon said, smiling. 'I've told you about myself but. . . .'

The man laughed. 'You think I look furtive? Here's my card if it gives you any help.' He handed Simon the card. On it was printed 'Dr Paul Orville' and an address in Geneva.

'Well, you hardly look like a family doctor. Maybe you

specialize in something?' Simon asked.

'I try not to publicize it.'

Simon grinned. 'Not an abortionist, are you?' He thought he could have done with his services once or twice in Malaya.

'No, I'm a psychiatrist. But, like you, I inherited some money, so I seldom practise now.'

'Why try and hide the fact?' Simon asked, leaning across the bar.

'Oh, once people know, they tend to pour out all their troubles, their whole damned life history. It becomes tedious.'

'Okay, let's do it the other way. Can you tell me something about myself, or is that the kind of thing you're trying to avoid?'

Dr Orville smiled. 'With this din going on and after a few drinks I'd doubt that I'd be very accurate.'

'I promise I have little to hide.'

Dr Orville looked away. 'The people who say that very often have the most to hide.' Simon gripped his glass tightly, then Orville stared at him. 'I'm not being rude, but very often people don't know what they're hiding. We are all driven by unconscious forces which we're not aware of. The iceberg is an example which is often cited. The shape, cracks, contours above the sea are a result of what is hidden below, about one-ninth of its volume, I believe. Most of us do not know who we really are.'

The doctor had struck a chord within Simon in his last phrase. The band had paused again, but the noise from the street had become almost as loud. Through the large glass windows they could see the silhouette of the mimosa shrubs that fringed the beach. There was no breath of wind. The ocean was so calm that all the lights of Agadir were reflected as in a mirror of black glass.

'It's the third day of Ramadan,' the doctor told him. 'They fast until sunset, then stay up all night and make up for it with a feast of mutton and semolina, kebabs and keftas, and huge pastries of honey and almonds. Those are very good,' he added.

Even here, the stray smell of spices and herbs drifted in from the still night air outside. Simon listened, then he reflected that the doctor had said he had never visited Morocco before. Perhaps

4

he had just memorized his guide book, but Simon felt uneasy; things didn't quite add up.

'You still haven't told me anything about myself,' he said, thinking he would call his bluff; perhaps the man wasn't a psychiatrist at all.

'Well, you're alone here in this hotel.'

'Yes . . . . How can you tell that?'

'I could give you reasons, but my assumption is based on an instinct one develops. I can't tell you why, because I don't know.'

'And what are these "reasons" of yours?'

'If your wife or your girlfriend were here you would be on the dance-floor. If she were ill in bed you wouldn't be likely to be in the bar at twenty-five minutes to twelve. But you'd rather not be alone because you're interested in pretty girls. I've seen your eyes flicker each time an attractive girl passed by . . . . You know, psychiatry is admittedly a question of knowing and understanding the basic principles. But in a way one is like a fortune teller – or like an oracle if you want to put the profession on a higher plane. It is partly intuition – call it what you will – and partly plain detective work . . . .'

'May I ask if you are married?' Simon enquired.

'I was,' Orville answered. 'My wife was killed in a car crash.'

'Why did you come to Agadir?'

Simon wondered why Orville hesitated for a moment.

'I'd read a travel book about Morocco, and I needed a holiday. I am what you might call a "loner". I've no children, no relations – and few friends. I'd read about Agadir, so I came here. Apparently you have to be south of the Atlas Mountains to be sure of sun at this time of year, and you can't be sure of it even then. I'm impressed by Agadir, with these beautiful squares, terraces and crescents. Of course, it is rather like Bournemouth, or even Nice, planted on an Atlantic beach. The Moroccans intend to make it another San Francisco, and they may well succeed, because the climate is perfect.'

The band began playing again, a waltz. Simon hoped it was the last.

Orville finished his drink. 'I'll give you a return drink tomorrow,' he told Simon. 'But now if you will excuse me I must go to bed.'

'Stay and have one more.' Simon felt suddenly frightened of being alone: it was absurd.

'You stay, and I'll tell the barman to chalk it up to me,' Orville said. 'I really am exhausted. It will be midnight in 20 minutes' time so I expect they will all be finishing shortly. I think I'll have another go at getting to sleep. See you tomorrow.' He spoke briefly to the barman and then turned back to Simon. 'Good night to you.'

Orville slid off his bar-stool and walked along the corridor towards the staircase.

Simon turned to the bar. The barman had his back to him; he was replacing a bottle of Campari. For a fraction of a second Simon saw in the mirror the starlit sky, as if the firmament and all the constellations had plunged down towards the earth; then he saw the bar split, the mirror, its bottles and glasses begin to fall and the barman himself, flinging his arms out, as if he alone could hold it, shrieking as he did so. At the same time there was a rumbling sound, more vast and deafening than thunder, like some great primeval groan which the earth was choking on, and in that moment, as Simon turned again, he saw the whole fabric of walls, ceiling, floor cracking open in the earthquake, shifting like jigsaw pieces, yet trembling. He rushed forward, hearing screams from the ballroom, shrieks of terror more piercing than any music, and curiously within that sound of human anguish the discordant chords of stringed instruments. Then they were plunged into darkness, but there was enough light from the sky to see Orville.

He had reached the staircase and he was running up it. Simon shouted. 'Come back, you fool. Get out of this place.' He began to run after him. 'The main door, get outside, it's our only chance.' But still Orville ran; he had now almost reached the top of the stairs and Simon began to follow him, still shouting but knowing no-one could hear him; for it seemed as if the hotel itself was being plucked out by its roots. He was thrown to the floor. The sound was deafening, as if some giant had straddled

6

the area, smashing glass windows, plucking iron girders from beneath the floors and tossing them into the sea, cracking stone and brick between his finger nails, brushing slates from roofs and trampling the fleeing people beneath his feet.

The sea hurtled against the broken windows. Simon, on his hands and knees, began to rise and then saw Orville again at the turn of the stairs, saw the staircase buckle, throwing Orville back and the marble landing heave, pulled into a distortion by the stairs and both collapsing, Orville between, hanging there for a moment clinging to the rail. Then the ceiling disgorged debris and there was nothing, nothing but dust, a red cloud, as if it were stained with blood.

Simon lurched towards the main door. He could see the sky and the stars moving, swinging back and forth, and as he moved he heard the final crescendo. He knew then it was the last, knew it would happen, that whatever he did he could not stop being buried alive. How many floors did the Hotel Saada have, he though with irony. The ceiling fell, a twisted mesh of metal; but then he was falling too, plunged into a deeper darkness than he had ever known.

Chapter 2

His head was stone, someone encased in the stone was knocking with an iron hammer. 'Get me out. I'll break my way out. I'm dead,' Simon thought. 'This is it, just pain and darkness and that stone.' His head was throbbing. He had had a dream of himself locked inside a stone slab, but now . . . he must open his eyes. His eyelids seemed stuck together, he forced the lids to open. Darkness. 'You must open your eyes,' he said. 'Try again.' Darkness. He listened. Silence.

'I'm still asleep, still dreaming, can I move? My right arm is jammed beneath me; something is pressing down across my chest; it's hard to breathe; my legs are pinioned. Jesus, help me. I must open my eyes. But they are open. Hell, this darkness can't exist: nothing can be as black as this.'

He could move his head a little, and his left hand was free. Slowly he lifted that hand and felt a pain at the back of his neck, but cautiously with his fingers as he explored the space, he felt the sharpness of twisted metal, something wooden across his chest, stone and rubble around him. He listened. Surely he would hear a sound, cries for help, masonry falling? But no, only this viscid darkness and a silence so unbearably soundless, he could have been the last man alive on earth.

'I probably am,' he thought sourly. 'If the hotel has collapsed it will take them days, even weeks, to get to me.' The thought of a slow death petrified him. Who said there would be rescuers anyway? The earthquake might have devastated the whole country. If only he was free to move, he would burrow a way out, yet which way? There was nothing he could do. Pray? Shout? He took a breath and called out. 'Help! Help!' Then he listened. That same terrifying silence.

Oh Christ, he thought, I'll believe in you, I'll do anything, if you only get me out of here. No, why should I lie again, not in the last hours of life. I won't make a bargain with a God I've never believed in. It would be like the same shabby deal that I've always fallen for. Can't I have some dignity, at the end of my life? Can't I be honest? 'Help!' he cried out again. 'Help.' The silence continued unbroken by even the faintest sound. Then he remembered that he had read somewhere that in a mining disaster one should not shout too often for fear of exhausting the oxygen.

He could feel his right arm growing numb; there was something trickling down his chest, blood or sweat, he couldn't tell.

He remembered that when he was a child, he had been playing with a door of a cupboard in his parents' living room when it had fallen over him; he was badly bruised, but the china ornaments inside the cupboard were smashed. His parents were furious, scolding him fiercely; they told him that the ornaments were the most valuable objects they had. He was plunged into guilt and remorse, but he also hated the ornaments, hated that they were loved when he was not.

Then there was the scout knife at school. He had found the knife in the playing fields. It had a screwdriver, a bottle-opener and four sharp blades with a horn handle edged with chromium. He knew that it must belong to someone in the school. Vaguely he remembered that he had seen a prefect called Lockwood using it. A week later a master had observed Simon with the knife and, realising that this must be the knife which Lockwood had reported missing, he accused Simon of stealing it. Simon's protestations that he had found the knife in the fields were not believed, but there was no evidence that he had stolen it. The knife was returned to Lockwood; but Simon knew himself to be branded as a liar and a thief.

Perhaps that's when it all started, he thought. Why should he care about being dug out, he wasn't worth it. At least he had been paid off to leave Malaya for good and had come to Africa, determined to change his life, to get a job, to become honest, maybe marry, settle down and have a family. He would love his kids, give them affection and concern, all the things his parents had refused him, too damned wrapped up in themselves to bother with an only child, he had just been an intrusion. Their death was instantaneous, not like this . . . don't think about death . . . think about anything. How long had he been here?

Kipling. The Barrack Room Ballads. Recite them to yourself. Dickens. Go over the plots. Had he dozed off? Lost consciousness? If only he knew the time. Okay, think about the early days in Malaya – those were good. The bribes weren't immoral, everyone took them, disguised as presents. Then there was Teena, her slim body was the colour of varnished oak, her black burnished hair smelt of orange blossom. He had bought her. He owned her, body and soul; she did whatever he wanted: she was his slave, she kissed his toes, licking his body languorously, slowly, adoringly with her pink tongue. For the first time he had felt a King. But he knew he couldn't marry her – that was taboo. Then she had left him and had become the mistress of a planter to the north, some sod with a double barrelled name. Taken for a ride again. Teena had never loved him. She had just used him as he had used her. Isabel, the wife of a planter on the next estate, had loved him. She played Chopin Nocturnes, played them delicately. Who would have thought with her fair hair and innocent blue eyes, that the other side of her was vulgar and mischievous? She hated the British snobs, the club life, the piddling rules of behaviour, hated her husband, 20 years older than her, hated all he stood for. What fun and joy they had had together, deceiving the whole lot of them, riding out together at dawn, lying in the shade, making love. But perhaps Isabel didn't hate them enough? In the end she chose wealth and security, chose to live on with that sour husband, for Simon was too poor; he had no future. Perhaps Isabel had not loved him enough, perhaps . . . he was just unlovable? The cupboard of his childhood – he had never forced himself free from it. This time the cupboard had fallen on him and there was no way out.

He could now feel a throbbing pain in his forehead and along his cheek. The air in his confined space stank of blood and sweat. Had he been trapped for several hours or longer, could it even be days? Perhaps he had been left for dead? His pain was growing unbearable. He tried to wriggle around to find some method of ending his life. He moved his left hand, then turned it around until he found a jagged edge of concrete. He now began to rub his left wrist up and down; this was one way of escaping, he could cut the vein in his wrist, and bleed to death. He began to twist his wrist to find the sharpest point of the concrete. At that moment he heard a voice. It was a French voice, '*On vient*,' he heard faintly. 'We're coming.' At first he thought it must be his imagination. '*Au secours!*' he called 'Help!'

Then he saw the first gleam of light. It came from a torch and it filtered dimly down to where he lay. From the right of him there came the noise of rubble and plaster being moved. As the light grew closer he could now see the situation he was in. Just above his head was poised a beam of concrete. By some freak this giant weight was held up only by a wooden chest. If it slipped he would be crushed to death. His rescuers worked with infinite caution, they had to move like miners in a three-foot seam in order to release him. He asked who they were, and they told him they came from the French Aero-Naval base 20 miles out of town, told him that it had not been touched by the earthquake which had completely devastated Agadir. Simon admired their bravery, for as they toiled the rubble above them was continually shifting, groaning as it moved. Slowly they eased the concrete beam away, then carefully dragged him towards them, passing him gently from sailor to sailor and out into the broken streets.

He looked about him. So it was still night. He asked the time. He had been buried for nearly 4 hours. He was in pain but felt tears stinging his eyes as they lifted him onto a stretcher. He expressed his thanks. What could he adequately say? Life was beautiful. He would never forget that. Yet the scene around him was horrific. A lament, a great wailing, seemed to reverberate among the broken stones and walls, and in the flickering light of flames he could discern figures desperately searching the rubble, women scrabbling in the dust and stones, banging their heads against a jutting beam, calling out in tears of anger. He saw small ragged children running through the crowds screaming hoarsely. The night sky was grey with dust, which covered the rescuers. A woman peered down at him, her face was streaked with tears. She murmured. 'My husband, in room 78, we were together when it happened. Room 78. Have you seen him?' Simon shook his head. 'We were together,' the woman went on, wringing her hands. 'How could we have been parted?'

The men lifted the stretcher into a van. 'Others are worse off,' one of them said. 'Some have lost their children.'

They drove to the emergency hospital at the Aero-Naval base outside the city. Fires burned in the ruined city. There was no building higher than one storey left; furniture littered the pavements and part of the road, an iron bedstead hung lopsidedly from a beam, a woman's arms hung limply through the rails. Simon saw another corpse flung over a joist like a suit of clothes. A grand piano lay upside down. A fire burned in the engine of a car, inside the driver's seat a man's face stared out blankly. The van stopped, the road was crowded with Moroccans, their white *djellabas* torn and stained, a bundle strapped to their mules, they dragged themselves along, moving without a sound except for a strange sigh, which seemed to emanate from their veiled women. 'In Ramadan, it is believed that one night is destined to mark the fate of man.' A voice spoke from the depths of the van. 'They have accepted their destiny. They will return to the mountains, to the old places they vacated in their youth. Allah has told them in this night.'

As the van moved on Simon felt in an obscure way that he had learned something significant too, but he could not clarify what it was. The hospital was full, the stretchers were laid outside in the gardens. Simon was placed next to a boy who cried out in sudden spasmodic outbursts, *'mes jambes . . . mes jambes . . . mon Dieu, Monsieur, s'il vous plait . . . .'* Simon looked; the boy had no legs, no legs at all. The sheet was bloodstained and flies were crawling over it. He turned away. A woman, her head swathed in bandages, came to every stretcher, she paused and asked urgently. 'Have you seen my little boy? He is only 3 years old, but he looks four. He has blond hair, and we call him Coco.' Nobody had seen him.

The road between Agadir and Casablanca had been cut by the earthquake; road transportation was impossible. But the French in Casablanca had organised an airlift by bombers which could land on the undamaged airfield.

The next day, Simon was carried to a bomber which was flying to Casablanca. On the stretcher next to him there lay a very young Moroccan girl. She was pregnant and badly cut about the head. Obviously, she had never flown before, for she trembled with fear. As the plane took off, Raschid, a young Moroccan male nurse knelt by the girl's side, put his hands on her sweating forehead, and whispered consoling words to her. It was several minutes before the girl realized she was unveiled. Roughly she brushed away Raschid's hand; he understood. Gently he reassured her that all was well and talked to her softly. He held her hand and wiped her brow. He soothed her as one might a wild bird caught in a net. Eventually the girl dozed off with her head on his lap. But as he knelt beside her Simon could see from Raschid's face that he was very cramped. Yet he never moved. Two hours after the plane landed in Casablanca she gave birth to a healthy baby.

The large French-organised hospital in Casablanca was crowded. At last Simon was given some morphine. When he awoke the following morning his head had been expertly bandaged and there was another bandage on one side of his face. But he could see and he could talk.

Raschid, seeing he was awake came over to him. 'How are we this morning?' he asked with a bright smile.

'A few aches and pains, bit stiff, but I think I feel almost okay.'

Raschid nodded. 'It was a miracle, you know. You were one of the lucky ones. We got you out because you were near the main door and they could burrow beneath the support beams.' He sighed. 'There are many in that hotel who are dead and others, still alive, but buried in the debris . . . .' He shook his head sadly and walked away down the ward.

Simon moved his arms, flexed the muscles in his legs: yes, a miracle. He drew in a large breath and exhaled. He lay back on the pillow and thought: so how can I give back to life what this experience has given me?

Yet as he went on thinking, he came to the conclusion that perhaps nothing had changed. He had few prospects, no job, no future, as Isabel had said so scornfully. Would he drift through the next few decades as he had done before?

The British Vice-Consul was making a tour around the hospital wards in which the casualties from Agadir had been placed. He stopped in front of Simon's bed and looked at a card at the end of it.

'There's no need to worry,' he said to Simon. He produced a torn leather despatch case from under his arm. 'Your despatch case with the travellers' cheques and the Letter of Credit has been found. I think, Dr Orville, you will discover that everything is present,' he continued, holding out the battered case. 'I hope you will find that there is nothing missing. Unfortunately I am afraid your medical case was smashed beyond recovery. Also your passport must have been left at the desk, which was destroyed completely. But when you are well enough to have your bandages removed I'll send a man round to do a passport photo of you.'

Simon had heard the words, heard the name, knew at once how the mistake had occurred, for they must have discovered Dr Orville's card in his wallet. Simon's passport had also been left at the reception desk. Yet as he was thinking this, he felt a strange sensation, almost as if some essential part of him had levitated. Was this the miracle, he wondered? Was he being given a new identity, a new personality, a new life, a new future, and indeed a new past? Was Simon Perry to be erased forever? Was he now the psychiatrist, Dr Orville? And from the sound of it, a rich and successful man? Anyone would be happy to slip into his dead shoes.

The Vice-Consul opened the despatch case. 'No doubt you're relieved to have this back,' he said, as he showed Simon the contents. 'Here are the travellers' cheques, £3,000 worth of them, and a Letter of Credit for nine thousand.'

The real Dr Orville was dead, there could be no doubt about that. Simon recalled that last glimpse of him, hanging for a second from the rail, the staircase buckling, Orville thrown, then crushed by the broken marble and masonry. This indeed must be what the Moroccans would call the voice of Allah himself speaking to him. And he remembered ironically that he had begun to pray to Jesus. Perhaps it made no difference. If fate or a God ordained the destiny of man, they had heard him refusing to lie, once in his life, and for that last gesture of self-respect they had now rewarded him.

The Vice-Consul was speaking again. 'There is one question that I would like to ask if you don't mind,' he said. 'May I ask why you are travelling with so much money? It seems an unusually large amount.'

Simon turned his bandaged head and tried to smile at the Vice-Consul. 'Because I am domiciled in Geneva,' he answered. 'I never know where my travels may take me, and I like to be well prepared. Besides, I had a vague idea of buying some little villa in these parts.' This seemed a good enough reason for Simon; it certainly convinced the Vice-Consul, who turned to go, then paused.

'If there is anything I can do for you, Dr Orville,' he said, 'let them know here at the hospital and they will telephone me. In the meantime I hope you will make a quick recovery.'

'Thank you,' he said to the Vice-Consul. 'I am most grateful.'

The Vice-Consul moved away, leaving Simon's thoughts in a turmoil. For some hours he could make no sense of what he had done. It had all seemed so easy. Yet it then struck him that he had allowed himself to be caught again. He had fooled himself about fate and Allah. What he had done was a criminal act. He had merely shown yet again that at heart he was a thief, taking money that didn't belong to him. And how the hell could he ever impersonate a psychiatrist? The whole episode was mad. Yet there was something grandly idiotic about it which had an irresistible appeal. Might he say, if he was found out, that in the earthquake, the shock or perhaps concussion had caused this aberration? Could he not be Dr Orville for a few days or weeks and then return to that frustrated, dismal failure, himself?

But as the days followed, and the hospital staff referred to him as doctor, giving him, he felt, special attention, the kind of respect and deference he had never had in all his life, the doctor's persona began to take hold of him. He had read about Freud and Jung, but never their original works; he had met rich women who had been psychoanalysed and he had thought it all one of the biggest con-tricks of the twentieth century. So if Dr Orville had made a fortune out of it, why should he not do the same? No, the whole idea was absurd. Besides, there was always a chance that someone might appear who had known Dr Orville. Therefore he must get out of Morocco as soon as he could. He remembered that Orville had told him he had flown to Agadir from Marrakesh: he had never visited Casablanca. His second problem was the signature on the travellers' cheques, but his right arm was damaged and a ligament had been torn and the arm was now in a sling, so this would excuse a signature unlike Orville's on each cheque. There was a third danger. When he was in Marrakesh, Orville might have gone to Wagon-Lits-Cook and a clerk behind the desk might have been transferred to Casablanca. But this was only one of the many difficulties that were present in his impersonation.

A day later the local French newspaper printed a list of the dead who had been in the Hotel Saada. The name of Simon Perry was included. Thus, to the outside world, Simon Perry was no longer alive.

The Moroccan authorities had announced that they intended to raze Agadir to the ground. Rescue teams and demolition squads were joined by disinfection workers because the peril from the town was now disease – rabies carried by infected dogs, typhus and bubonic plague. Tons of quicklime were brought to be scattered over the ruins which were now being flattened by bulldozers. Even so, over a week after the catastrophe, survivors were still being rescued from under the rubble. Voluntary work camps had been formed to help the refugees. Red Cross workers organised them. But the old kasbah on the hill overlooking Agadir had been totally destroyed. Hundreds of bodies had been bulldozed into the earth. Agadir as a town was now dead. Simon Perry, as man, was also dead.

Chapter 3

Raschid was extremely helpful; he arranged for Simon's suit to be patched up and cleaned. With the money that Simon still had in his pocket Raschid bought him a shirt, pyjamas, shaving kit and a hold-all.

Simon asked him for advice about finding a quiet hotel in Casablanca in which he could stay while he made his arrangements to leave Morocco. Raschid suggested the Hotel Atlantique.

'It is not a popular hotel,' he said. 'But it is quiet and comfortable.' On the day of his departure from hospital Simon gave Raschid some money as a present; they parted sadly. Simon was now on his own.

He took a taxi to the Hotel Atlantique, and left his bag in the room Raschid had booked for him. From that moment onwards he had worked out his plans. He left the hotel, went out into the street and found a taxi and asked the driver to go to Wagon-Lits-Cook.

He was amazed at the crowds, the complex mixture, the colour, the noise, all the horns of all vehicles seemed to be blaring at once. Motor cyclists accelerated, turning and twisting through the traffic. A tall Arab in a gauzy *djellaba* was lecturing to a group of tourists on the steps of a huge, gleaming white building. Yet many Moroccans wore suits with the *djellabas* open and flowing behind. They looked trim and smart with their neat moustaches and red fez; others wore turbans. With their hawk noses and full beards they looked as if they had stepped from the pages of the Old Testament; their heavily veiled women, three paces behind, carried the luggage. In the midst of all this prosperity there were beggars in dirty rags asking for alms, their faces covered in scabs, thrusting out their deformities to the passing people. There were peasants sitting side-saddle on their mules, kicking the mangy flanks with their heels, indifferent to the traffic around them.

The streets were lined with high grandiose buildings; the ground floors were shops, filled with imported cameras and watches; filled with diverse luxury articles at high prices. And everywhere, it seemed to Simon, there were banks, decorated with a profusion of Islamic motifs and stucco arabesques, banks with Moorish arches leaping upwards to the startling blue sky like vast wedding cakes of finance. Was it just these tall buildings which increased his nervousness, fearful of another earthquake? Or was it his plan, which he now began to distrust? No, if he could leave Morocco, then he would be safe.

They reached Wagon-Lits-Cook.

His right arm was still in a sling, but he could move his fingers in a shaky imitation of Orville's signature on each cheque. He was carrying his new passport in his breast pocket. He walked into the office. His only risk, as he had known, was that some clerk from the Marrakesh office might have been transferred. He produced his passport and his travellers' cheques and was directed to the exchange counter.

'I was in the Agadir earthquake,' he explained to the clerk behind the desk. 'So I'm afraid that my signature looks a bit odd, but here is my passport.' The Moroccan clerk glanced at the passport with the new photograph the Consulate had issued to Simon and then smiled at him.

'I want £1,000 in Moroccan currency and £1,000 in dollars please,' Simon told him. The clerk watched him as he counter-signed each cheque, then he took the cheques and Simon's passport and disappeared into the far end of the room. Simon tried to control his nerves as he waited. It seemed a long wait. Suddenly from the cashier's desk a polite voice called out, 'Dr Orville.'

For an instant Simon hesitated, then he realized he was being summoned. He walked slowly towards the cashier's desk. The clerk was there holding Simon's passport and his money which the cashier counted out for him. Simon could feel the sweat trickling down his sides. With his left hand he collected his passport and his money. He thanked the clerk and the cashier and moved towards the shipping counter. The first stage of his plan had been successful.

At the shipping counter he looked through their leaflets and finally booked himself on a cargo boat sailing in 3 weeks' time from Casablanca to Vera Cruz on the east coast of Mexico. He decided to spend this interval in one of the remote villages in the Rif Mountains. After he had made the booking for his passage and paid for it he walked out of the office; he decided he needed a drink. He went to a café off the main boulevard and ordered a large brandy and a sandwich. He noticed his hand was trembling. But he had taken the risk; now there could be no turning back. He walked into the main boulevard, found a large store and entered it. First he bought a suitcase; next he bought all the clothes he would need for the journey to Mexico and put them into his new case.

There were no taxis, so he decided to return to the Hotel Atlantique on foot. He could cut through some back streets, he knew it wasn't far if you avoided the main boulevards. Casablanca was nothing like the film, he thought, but then that had been a mock-up set in the studio. *Play it again Sam.* Play what again, Dr Orville? In Mexico, you'll need the Letter of Credit. How long will that keep you? What is the set-up in Geneva? Orville said he didn't practise any more. But did he live alone? Did he have a house, an apartment, a housekeeper perhaps? Would not someone, in a few weeks' time, make an enquiry as to why Dr Orville had not returned from Morocco? Then through the Letter of Credit they were bound to trace him.

Moroccans were staring at him as he passed tiny shops and stalls crammed close together: they pestered him with articles, silk scarves, beads, jewellery, copperware, leather goods, pushing the stuff in front of him, running after him. They smelt of sweat and spices and shouted at him in a mixture of French and Arabic. He reached the entrance of the hotel, exhausted; he held his jacket in his hand, his shirt clung damply to his body.

As he arrived at the desk he was greeted by the receptionist. 'Good afternoon, Dr Orville,' the clerk said.

At that moment a man got up from a chair in which he was sitting in the murky depths of the hall and advanced towards Simon. The man was well-built and of medium height; he looked virile and powerful, but there was something flabby about his face. Though he was still young, about 30, he reminded Simon of a boxer who had gone to seed. He was a Moroccan, but he was dressed in smart clothes which probably came from Paris or Rome. On his wrist he wore a slim gold watch and on the other an identity disc held in position by a heavy gold chain.

'Good day, Dr Orville,' the man said, speaking with a slight American accent.

Immediately Simon grew tense; he hid his alarm as best he could.

'I'm glad that we have met at last. But why did you come to this place?' the man continued. 'The hotel where we had arranged to meet is far more comfortable. Never mind. Perhaps you now prefer a smaller hotel after the Agadir earthquake. We had no idea that you had gone to stay in Agadir before meeting us in Casablanca. It came as quite a shock when we saw your name as one of the survivors.' He paused as if waiting for Dr Orville to say something.

'I was lucky to get out alive,' Simon muttered. 'But how did you find out that I was in this hotel?'

'That was quite simple,' the man explained. 'I went round all the hospitals where the wounded had been taken. And at your hospital I was lucky enough to meet Raschid, the young orderly, who told me that he had advised you to stay in this hotel if you wanted to rest. However, thanks to Allah, we have met at last. And I must tell you that Mrs Morrison simply can't wait to meet you. She was delighted when you wrote from Geneva accepting her offer. The job isn't very difficult – as you will see for yourself. Have you eaten?'

'Yes,' Simon replied.

'Please forgive me,' the man said with a pleasant smile. 'You must excuse my manners, but I was so excited to meet you that I forgot to introduce myself. My name is Tariq ben Kassim, but at the villa they call me Toni – with an "i". I run Betty Morrison's affairs for her. So now let's go. I'll tell the porter to take your suitcase to my car which is waiting outside.'

Simon could see a noose dangling ahead of him. For all his charm, Toni looked as if he could be a dangerous enemy. Simon was determined that somehow he must get free of him. He asked the concierge for the key to his room.

'I've just got to collect some odds and ends which I've got upstairs,' he explained.

'But I thought you had just checked in,' Toni said.

'No, I checked in earlier,' Simon told him. 'You see, I lost most of my clothes in the earthquake, and I've been out shopping. I'll go upstairs to my room and pop them into the suitcase I've just bought.'

Toni spoke in Arabic to the porter who took Simon's suitcase and moved towards the lift.

'I'll come upstairs with you,' Toni announced. He gave a short laugh. 'Now I've found you,' he said, 'I don't intend to let you out of my sight.'

The porter opened the lift door. 'After you,' Toni said to Simon with an eloquent gesture. Toni followed him into the lift. It was evident he did not intend to leave him alone. Did he suspect his identity, Simon wondered. He gave no signs of doing so. But what was the job, and who was Betty Morrison? Was he expected to try to cure the mental derangement of Mrs Morrison or someone in the villa? He must get away from them as soon as he could. Meanwhile all he could do was to let Toni escort him to the villa. Once there, he must escape.

Outside Simon's hotel room the porter opened the door with the master key. The room was small and square and communicated with a bathroom. The stained marble floor was strewn with brightly coloured Moroccan rugs. Without thinking, Simon moved towards the Moorish window. He gazed down at the street below. For a wild moment he considered trying to jump out of the window. Then he rejected the idea as being ridiculous. He stared across the many flat roofs, pierced by minarets with green and golden domes. He had heard the *muezzin's* cry, he had seen a white haired man in the crowds, soundlessly chanting, gesturing with his arms, like one in a trance. But Simon did not belong. He was trapped, or had he trapped himself?

A large white Mercedes was parked in front of the hotel entrance. The porter had put Simon's hold-all and suitcase into the boot. Toni opened the door at the front of the car for Simon and then went round and got into the driver's seat.

'I drive fast,' he warned Simon, 'but I'm a very good driver.' The car moved swiftly through the outskirts of the town, taking the coast route towards Essaouira. The sea glittered in the bright sunshine. The Atlantic waves rolled slowly, foaming as they reached the shore.

As they passed the large *bidonvilles* Toni glanced at Simon, who had been staring at them in dismay: shelters made from old oil drums, a few planks and tattered blankets; women and children sitting on dirt floors, their faces blank, yet their dark eyes glaring with defiant hatred.

'We have had independence for only a few years,' Toni said, 'but already we have begun to clear away these wretched areas where the poor live, and we are building decent working blocks for them. In 5 years' time Morocco will be one of the finest countries in the world.'

Simon thought him naïve. Poverty stank, it was ingrained in humanity; he recognized part of himself there.

After an hour they passed through a decrepit village which seemed to have only one petrol station and one café with dingy little single-storeyed shops between them. They turned left across a flat plain which was partly cultivated and led in the direction of some distant hills. On the roadside, lined in places with eucalyptus trees, they could now see flocks of goats tended by skinny little boys, and camels attached to make-shift ploughs digging up the soil. Peasants sitting sideways on their donkeys on a narrow track moved patiently between the trees. Beside the road were now clustered small *douars* – tiny hamlets surrounded by thick hedges of prickly pear.

'Is it a long drive to Mrs Morrison's villa?' Simon asked.

'Not far,' Toni replied. 'I can generally do it in two hours. Luckily these roads weren't affected by the earthquake. It must have been a nightmare,' Toni continued. 'From your forehead it looks as if your injuries must have been quite serious.'

Simon's right arm was aching, and he decided to take off the sling which was cramping him. He tossed it into the back of the car.

'It was terrible,' he answered. For a moment he remembered the earthquake vividly. 'But what made it less ghastly was the wonderful way in which people behaved – the wounded and the orderlies and the doctors. The airlift by bombers from Agadir to various hospitals in Morocco was a great achievement.' Simon was thinking in particular of Raschid and the little Moroccan girl.

Toni nodded. They drove in silence for several minutes.

'When I first met Betty Morrison,' Toni said, 'she was living with her daughter Caroline at the Minzah Hotel in Tangier. They didn't like the climate. She wanted a villa which was both large and remote. So we moved south and eventually found this crumbling old villa which had once been a palace. Betty spent a small fortune getting the place habitable, and last year we moved in.'

Simon would have liked to ask many questions, but he was afraid, so he was silent.

Mrs Morrison was bound to know the real Dr Orville, so there was about an hour left before he would be discovered as a fraud. So why was he sitting here, being driven through this dry landscape with its thin layer of soil over grey rock and the tireless peasants scratching a living from it? Toni pointed out a *marabout's* tomb, a square block with a small whitewashed dome. 'Even in death, they believe him to be a benign influence, for the tomb still radiates his *baraka.*'

Simon glanced behind him, pink oleanders shielded the tomb. He silently prayed that the *marabout's baraka* might sustain him. Perhaps this Mrs Morrison had never met the real Orville? But why ask a stranger to your home? Toni was intent on not allowing him out of his sight. Suppose he suggested they stop at the next village and he asked to stretch his legs? He would have to leave the briefcase, Toni would be bound to accompany him anyway. No, there was little hope; he would have to get to the villa and pray. *Baraka* or not, he must play it all by ear.

Suddenly a question came into his mind. 'How do you come to speak such good English?' he asked.

'My parents were rich,' Toni told him. 'My father was a banker in Rabat. He was very strict. There was an old English woman who came each day to teach me English, and if she told my parents that I had been slack in my lessons, my father would beat me. Then his bank went broke, and my parents moved to a little farm they had bought in the country.'

Toni seemed to be very friendly, and eager to talk. Simon nodded to encourage him.

'Life there was very dull,' Toni continued, 'and my father was more strict than ever. But I was now fourteen. Like most boys of my age I wanted adventure and excitement, so I saved up the little pocket money they gave me. One night I left the farm and caught an early morning bus to Tangier.'

Toni smiled at Simon. 'Do you know Tangier?'

'No,' Simon answered after a pause. 'I've never been to Morocco before.'

'They tell me it's different now,' Tony said. 'But in the days when it was an International Zone, it wasn't difficult for a young boy to make money. I soon learned how to go about it.' Toni smiled at Simon apologetically. 'Late one night I met a Frenchman who took me back to his apartment. I stayed the night with him. I liked him, and he was very gentle with me. In the morning he informed me that I would never make good money by roaming the streets late at night. He told me that he ran an expensive bar for men. His customers were very rich – mainly French, American and English, and they paid a lot of money to have a boy for an hour or two. That's quite an accepted thing in Morocco. He told me that if I came and stayed in his apartment I could go to his bar when it opened at seven in the evening. He was certain that I would be picked up by 9 o'clock, and later I could go back and spend the night with him.'

Toni glanced at Simon. 'I hope I'm not shocking you,' he said.

'Not in the least,' Simon replied. 'But you make it all sound so easy.'

Toni laughed. 'It *was* easy — if you had good looks and were well-built and prepared to do anything. Of course I wasn't particular. To please myself I would sometimes go with a woman. If she was very nice I wouldn't ask her for money. But after a time I began to get a bit fed up with the life I was leading, and I got a job as a member of the crew of one of the smugglers' motor-boats that ran from Tangier to Barcelona and Marseilles. The crew was very well paid. But after a few trips the police got on to us, and it looked as if I was going to be sent to prison. I had already met Betty, and I went to her with all my troubles. She was wonderful. I have no idea how much money she paid to the police. She will never tell me. But I knew I was safe so long as I was with Betty, and her daughter didn't seem to mind. By then I had got fond of Betty. I've been with her ever since.'

Simon had been surprised and interested by Toni's obvious frankness in telling the story of his youth. Once again he longed to know who the patient was in the villa whom he was supposed to help, but he knew that he must be constantly careful not to betray his ignorance of the situation in the place.

Toni turned the car into a smaller road that wound up a hill. 'You can see the villa now,' Toni announced, pointing to the left.

Half way up the hill Simon could see the crenellated walls, terracotta in colour, which evidently formed a compound in the centre of which was the villa, three storeys high, with Moorish windows and an ornamental façade. The villa was certainly large; Simon looked at the height of the walls in dismay. They now approached an imposing gate made of wrought iron. As the car drew up to the gate it was opened by an old Moroccan who was obviously the watchman. The car stopped at a wide flight of steps that led up to the front door. Two servants wearing tunics and Moorish pantaloons greeted them. Toni spoke to them briefly in Arabic, then turned to Simon.

'The servants will look after your things,' he said. 'If you don't mind I'll show you the way.'

Simon followed Toni up the flight of steps, through a hall with fretted woodwork descending from the domed ceiling, and along a corridor leading to a heavy door which Toni opened.

'Could you wait in here?' he asked, as they entered a long, spacious room.

Chapter 4

Simon's first impression was of whiteness. The walls, the curtains, the sofas and armchairs were all white.

Toni had left the room and as Simon's eyes now became accustomed to the shaded area, he saw that the tiled floor was covered in Persian and Afghan rugs. At the end of the room there was a large desk inlaid with mother-of-pearl, ebony and lemonwood, in an intricate Islamic design. He felt the drawers, they were locked. He crossed over to the windows, opened one shutter, and peered out. Tall cedar trees masked the view, but he thought he could catch a glimpse of mountains flecked with gold in the sun. Why was he waiting here? Was he being watched? He had an uneasy feeling that behind the intricate grilles which marked one wall, someone was peering at him. Why had he tried the drawers of the desk?

He sat down in a deep armchair and lit a cigarette. He was thirsty: he needed a drink badly. It was then that the door opened and a plump, elegantly dressed woman entered. He estimated her age as 50 and noticed that both powder and lipstick had been freshly applied, her perfume was strong. He had already risen, waiting in that moment for her furious rejection of him, but she still walked across the room, extending a hand, swollen with rings, and smiling. 'Dr Orville?' she enquired.

He felt a surge of relief. His bladder seemed so full that the pain was immense. 'Yes, Paul Orville,' he heard himself saying.

'I'm Betty Morrison,' the woman said. 'I must tell you I'm delighted that you are here. We were very worried when we heard you had been in Agadir.' Betty turned towards another woman about her own age who had also come into the room. 'And now I'll introduce you to my secretary . . . Sheila,' she said in a tone of command, 'come and meet Dr Orville.'

The secretary walked up to him and shook his hand.

'Sheila Adams,' she murmured. Her smile was false: it sat uneasily on her over-painted features. 'I'm glad to meet you.'

'Toni, will you show Dr Orville to his room? But please don't be long. I have so much I want to discuss with you,' Betty Morrison said.

Toni had appeared in the doorway. Simon nodded to the two women and gratefully left them, assuring them that he would return within 10 minutes. Toni led the way up a tiled stairway and down a long corridor bisected with carved and painted arches. Simon noticed several wooden doors with their panels inlaid and decorated; the labyrinth design was almost overpowering in its detail. Yet this was nothing compared to his own room; Toni opened the door and inclined his head, pointing to the bathroom which lay beyond the huge space smelling of musk and camphor. Upon a dais stood a brocade draped bed, further obscured by a cloud of mosquito netting. The high-ceilinged roof had tile mosaics on the lower walls and plaster friezes which climbed up to the coffered ceiling. The floor was tiled in diamonds of turquoise and yellow, even the furniture was carved and painted; mirrors with frames of scarlet wood reflected all the colours with kaleidoscopic bravura. Simon crossed the room to the bathroom, noticing that his bags had been placed in one corner. He released the tension in his bladder, and lent his forehead against the tiled wall. At least the bathroom was more sober, he thought, and wondered what situation he had got himself stuck into. This Morrison woman looked as if she was the Woolworth heiress. Well, with luck, if he played along with style, he might come out of it all with even more money than he dared hope. He glanced at his watch. Five minutes had gone by. He washed his hands, threw cold water onto his face, and going back into the bedroom he walked over to the windows. They were covered in an intricate wrought-iron design. He unlatched them and then the white shutters. He noticed that he had a balcony which overlooked a garden, a paved patio and another separate part of the house which was covered in a profusion of purple bougainvillea. He supposed them to be the servants' quarters. He could have tried to escape now, yet his curiosity was aroused. Mrs Morrison had accepted him as the psychiatrist, the great stumbling block was over. He walked back to the main drawing room feeling more assured.

Betty was talking in a low voice to Toni at the other end of the room. He paused in the doorway and Betty turned at once. She crossed to the sofa and beckoned Simon to sit beside her. 'What will you drink?' she asked him. 'We've got almost anything you can think of.'

'Thanks,' Simon said. 'I'd like a whisky and soda.'

'So should I,' Betty said. 'Toni, be an angel and fix our drinks.' The tone of her strangely vibrant voice contained a mixture of affection and command.

Toni opened a long Chinese lacquered cabinet which contained a bar.

'I'd ask you to stay with us, Toni, my dear,' Betty said to him as he poured out their drinks. 'But you do understand that I must be left alone with Dr Orville for a while. Besides, you've heard me talking about most of it already. And you know how things stand.'

'I certainly do,' Toni replied. 'You can get me on the intercom if you want anything.' He handed them the drinks. 'I'll leave you now,' he announced. 'Good luck to you both.'

'I don't know what I'd do without Toni,' Betty said after the door had closed behind him. 'He's been with me for some time now. He runs all my affairs, and I suppose you could say that he runs me. But you haven't come all the way from Geneva to hear about my relationship with my darling Toni. You've come to give my daughter Caroline treatment. It's Caroline we must talk about.'

Now Simon realized the purpose of his visit.

He felt an abyss of self-doubt enclose him. How could he possibly pretend to be a psychiatrist when he had only the vaguest notions of what they did? But wasn't one of their methods just to allow the patients to talk? Didn't they just sit in a dimly lit room while their patients lay on a sofa and spilled out

29

their fears, dreams, and aspirations? That couldn't be difficult. And hadn't he also vaguely heard that patients always fell in love with their psychiatrists? That might even be fun. He nodded and smiled at Betty as she continued to talk.

'I tried to explain part of the problem in my brief letters to you. But thank heavens we are now alone together, and I can talk freely ... I suppose it best I should tell this story from scratch which will at least fill in the gaps between my letters to you. To begin with, Henry Morrison, who was an extremely wealthy New York property broker – what we'd call an Estate Agent. In 1929 he married a girl called Mary-Lou Brownlee. Henry was then 32, Mary-Lou was just twenty. In 1930 a son was born, and they christened him Clifton. But after the birth of Clifton, Mary-Lou began to loathe her husband. From all accounts she was a pretty good bitch. Slowly the two of them grew further and further apart, and of course she influenced her son against his father. Early in 1938, Henry was divorced by Mary-Lou. She retained custody of the boy.'

Betty re-filled her glass from the bar in the cabinet and went on talking.

'Immediately after Mary-Lou's divorce,' Betty continued as she sat down again on the sofa, 'Henry Morrison sailed to England. In London he met little me at a cocktail party. I was at the time acting as private secretary to a dress designer. Henry took a fancy to me right away. He took me out to dinner quite often, and we went to lots of places together. I was wildly attractive in those days – believe it or not – and Henry was quite handsome in his way. We became lovers. Then I got pregnant and we married. Our daughter Caroline was born early in 1939. Just before the outbreak of war, Henry took Caroline and I back to New York. So Caroline grew up in America – though we visited England occasionally after the war ended. I must tell you that as a child Caroline was highly strung. She was so nervous that it seemed impossible to send her away to school, and she was educated by a series of tutors and governesses. She stayed most of the time on Henry Morrison's estate in Connecticut. I must also tell you that Caroline takes a great deal after my own mother – who had to

30

spend the last years of her life in what was politely termed a "rest home". Caroline certainly inherited her grandmother's good looks.'

Betty was silent for a moment, but her heavily be-ringed hand moved almost incessantly, gesturing, stroking the side of her glass of whisky, tapping on the arm of the sofa. And Simon noticed her slightly protuberant eyes and a look of suppressed fear, even hysteria. She now scrabbled in a silver box for a cigarette which she held out for Simon to light.

'In the meantime,' she went on, 'Caroline's half brother, Clifton Morrison, was growing up into a thoroughly wild and unruly young man. During the Korean war he served briefly in Korea, but he was invalided out of the army with suspected tuberculosis. While he was in the Far East, Clifton developed an interest in the so-called mystic religions. I know that he spent at least one leave in Japan, visiting shrines at Kyoto.

'As I told you, Mary-Lou had always encouraged Clifton to despise his father. And when he came back to America, after his medical discharge from the army, Clifton made a point of doing all he could to annoy Henry, although he was fond of him. For instance, he read revolutionary mish-mash and left the books lying about the New York apartment so Henry would see them. Clifton soon adopted a mental attitude of living for kicks – from one moment to the next. Gradually he came under the sway of the Beat Movement with its strange mixture, as you probably know, of cultural influences, Eastern religions, drugs, jazz, poetry by Ginsberg and books by Jack Kerouac. In 1955 when he was aged twenty-five Clifton was arrested and charged with being in possession of marijuana. I went to Henry and managed to persuade him to help. I can tell you this – it was only Henry's money and influence which saved Clifton from a court appearance and a prison sentence. As soon as all that trouble was over, Henry tried to reason with Clifton. He offered to take him into his firm. But to no avail. Clifton didn't want to know. In a way, Henry was fond of his son, however much he was disappointed in him. But by now Clifton was getting on his nerves and seemed a hopeless case. So he gave the young man $25,000 and asked him to stay away and not to worry him any longer. Henry worked himself into a rage which I knew he regretted later. He told Clifton that as far as he was concerned he was no son of his, and he never wanted to see him again. A few months' later Henry was sorry he had been so harsh. He tried to get in touch with his son. But Clifton had left America. We had no address for him. However, we heard rumours that he had gone back to the Far East. Three years later Henry had a fatal stroke.'

Once again Betty rose from the sofa and walked with her quick little steps to the cabinet to refill her glass. 'What about you?' she asked Simon. 'Come and help yourself.' Simon rose and went to pour himself another drink.

'Here comes the difficult part,' Betty said when they were settled on the sofa. 'When Henry's Will was read, it was discovered that the bulk of his fortune had been left in trust to Caroline – with the proviso that Caroline was completely sane on her twenty-first birthday which, as I told you in a letter, falls very soon now. So we have only until the end of the week to prepare her for her ordeal. Two doctors are flying from New York to examine her. If they decide that she is not completely sane the money will pass to Clifton. So there is where you come in, Dr Orville. As I told you in my first letter, I heard from a friend of mine that you've got this new wonderful drug that calms the nerves completely while still leaving the mind alert. What's more, after 8 hours there's no trace of it. And now the day of decision is drawing close.'

Betty's quivering hand was moving up and down the arm of the sofa. 'I forgot to tell you that Henry left me quite a nice sum of money and the New York apartment. But it seemed to me that it was far more sensible to sell the New York apartment, get rid of the saleable assets, and move to a less expensive spot. We first went to Tangier, but the place was very humid, and there were weeks on end when you didn't see a glimmer of sunshine. It was in Tangier that we met Toni who has been a wonderful help ever since. I simply don't know what I would have done without him. First of all he drove us to Casablanca in my Mercedes, and we began to tour the country to the south where there is more sunshine. This villa seemed the perfect place, and so it has proved to be.'

Betty was silent for a moment. Simon decided that it was time he said something.

'And how is Caroline?' he asked.

'Well, that is a problem we've got to face,' Betty said. 'She can be a sweet girl – though she's a bit aloof at times. Her history of these hallucinations, which are sometimes quite severe, goes back into childhood. She has had several psychiatrists who have given her treatment, and sometimes I believe she has been cured. I don't think, Dr Orville, your task is impossible because my lawyers have explained what the legal requirement is.'

Betty paused and scrutinized him. 'The law defines sanity quite differently from the medical profession.'

'Oh yes,' Simon murmured, thinking what the hell could that be? He avoided Betty's eyes.

'You know?' she asked.

He lighted a cigarette, there was a slight pause, then he turned to Betty and said, smiling, 'Remind me.'

'The two specialists have to prove that Caroline is mentally incompetent to manage the estate which she'll inherit,' Betty said. 'They can't just say because she sometimes has, or seems to have, these hallucinations, that she is suffering from a mental disorder. They have to prove that the mental disorder causes an impairment of judgement which would make her incapable of managing her very large fortune.'

'I see. May I ask your own opinion?' Simon said.

'It's so difficult for me to judge.' Betty sighed. 'She is erratic. For instance, on some days she will only eat food she has prepared herself because she's afraid some unknown person is trying to poison her. She is also acutely suspicious of men. But why she is I can't imagine, because at no stage in her life has there been any unpleasantness involving a man. But what worries me most is that she doesn't seem to want to meet anyone. She says she's happier living alone. So we've fixed up a complete apartment for her which is separate from the house. Sometimes she comes over to eat with us, and sometimes she has her meals in her own little

33

dining-room. I should also tell you, Dr Orville, that she has recently been suffering from a particular hallucination. But I wonder about this. When she told me about it I suspected that it was only a ploy to draw attention to herself. However, I'm sure you will be able to persuade her to tell you what has been disturbing her. And of course I'm sure that you will warn Caroline of the danger of discussing her hallucinations with the doctors who come for their examination on her 21st birthday.'

Suddenly Betty's eyes seemed more protuberant than ever. 'As I said in one of my letters, what I paid you is only half of your final fee,' she told him. 'If Caroline is declared legally competent on her birthday, I've got the remainder of your fee in cash. It is in the safe in my bedroom. And the whole amount, I'm sure you will admit, is a very large fee for a week's work. However, I have confidence in you. I think you will like Caroline, and I believe she will like you. I want you to win her confidence. I want you to impress on my daughter how careful she must be as to what she says at her examination. I want her to be what she is already when she's in a good state of mind – and that is a very charming and perfectly balanced young girl. And I am certain that what my friend called your "wonder drug" together with your general treatment will do the trick. I presume you've brought the drug with you?'

Simon hesitated. Then he remembered that on his discharge from the hospital in Casablanca he had been issued with a large bottle of the mild sleeping tablets he had been taking for the pains in his head as a result of the injury.

'Yes,' he said. 'I packed the bottle in cottonwool. The drug is in tablet form and in good condition. From all you tell me I think I can say that I'm sure I can help Caroline. You can be assured I'll do my best.'

Simon leaned back on the sofa. His immediate task, he decided, was not going to be very difficult. Before now he had met hysterical girls who had lost all form of self-control because they had been so badly spoiled. The doctors were not coming for another 5 days, Simon thought to himself, during which time he would try to make his escape.

'I've talked enough,' Betty said. 'Let's finish our drinks, and I will take you to Caroline's apartment to introduce you.'

Chapter 5

Betty led the way into the patio which his own room overlooked. On one side he could glimpse an oval swimming pool through large shrubs of poinsettias, great calla lilies and trailing geraniums; on his right there was a tall brick wall with a small door shaped like a keyhole in it. The wall was covered in honeysuckle and blue morning glory. Betty walked up a flight of marble steps that led onto a terrace and knocked on a white painted door.

'Caroline,' she called out. 'Can we come in?'

'I suppose so,' replied a distant voice.

Betty opened the door and they walked into Caroline's living-room. The curtains were made from light blue silk, the sofa and chairs were white, scattered with blue and green cushions; the pictures on the walls were by Marie Laurençin and Odilon Redon. Somehow everything seemed to blend harmoniously together. The French windows at the end of the room opened out onto a broad balcony on which, lying on a heavily upholstered beach-chair, was Caroline. Two brightly-coloured umbrellas shaded her from the afternoon sun. She was wearing green silk trousers and a white shirt. She was very slender. With her long hair, slim face and large hazel-coloured eyes Simon decided she was extremely attractive. Then he remembered his rôle as a psychiatrist and looked at her more intently. She was very pale and wore almost no make-up. There was a strained look about her face.

As they advanced Caroline turned her head towards them.

'Caroline dear,' Betty said. 'This is Dr Orville. He is a very kind man, and I'm sure you'll get on well together.'

For the first time Simon noticed that Betty's voice was slurred. She had probably been drinking before he and Toni had arrived.

'Caroline dear,' Betty repeated. 'This is Dr Orville.'

Caroline ignored Simon, and spoke to her mother. 'Tell him to get out,' she said in a flat voice.

'Caroline,' Betty said in reproach, 'Dr Orville has come all the way from Geneva to see you.'

'I don't care whether he has come from Timbuktu. I don't want to see him,' Caroline replied.

'Well, you're seeing him now,' Betty pointed out. 'And I insist you get to know each other. He's already promised that he won't stay long with you.'

'He won't if I have anything to do with it,' Caroline answered.

'Now that's no way to behave,' Betty said, walking to the door with her short steps which were now a little unsteady. 'I'm going to leave the two of you together whether you like it or not.' Then she swayed out of the room closing the door behind her.

For a while there was silence.

They were watching each other cautiously. Simon kept trying to put himself in the role of a psychiatrist, but he could not help being aware that Caroline had very smooth skin. With her tilted nose which was slightly too broad and her wide mouth, she looked like the spoiled girl he had imagined – but more beautiful. Caroline was staring at him.

'Are you a psychiatrist?' she asked.

'Yes,' Simon replied with a slight smile which he hoped would be reassuring.

'I suppose you want to ask me a lot of stupid questions?' Caroline asked. She spoke with a faint American accent.

'Not if you don't want to answer them,' Simon replied. 'I'm not going to drag any confessions out of you.'

'That's what they all say,' Caroline answered.

'But I mean it,' Simon said.

Still staring at him, Caroline sat upright in the chair. 'Care for a drink?' she enquired.

Simon hesitated. He glanced at the drink-trolley and saw it was full. 'I'd like a whisky and soda,' he said.

'Alcoholism isn't one of my problems,' Caroline told him. 'But

I'll have an orange juice if you'll pour me one. Help yourself to what you want.'

'Thanks,' Simon said, approaching the drink-trolley. He poured out an orange juice from a tall jug with ice in it and mixed himself a large whisky and soda. He was beginning to feel nervous again; he also felt strangely excited.

Simon raised his glass. 'Your very good health,' he said to her. 'And I intend to see in these next few days that you *have* good health.'

Again there was silence.

'Do you mind if I sit down?' Simon asked.

'No,' Caroline replied.

'Thank you,' Simon said and sat down. Caroline was still hostile, he decided. But at least she was now talking to him.

'You don't look like a psychiatrist,' Caroline remarked.

Simon smiled. 'But I can assure you that I am,' he answered. 'What makes you think I'm not?'

Caroline looked at him carefully. 'There's nothing I've noticed in particular,' she replied. 'I expect it's my imagination. But somehow you don't give me the *impression* of being a psychiatrist.'

Well, she was right there, he thought. He stared into his glass.

'What would you like to tell me?' Simon asked.

'Actually, I wouldn't *like* to tell you anything. I've told it all before. A hundred times. And I'm fed up with it. However, I'm perfectly prepared to answer any questions you want to ask me as long as they are intelligent. But, as I said, let there be as few questions as possible, because I'm tired of answering them.'

'Then don't bother yourself,' Simon said. 'Don't let's have any questions. I'm quite happy to sit here in the sun drinking whisky.'

Caroline leaned forward. 'But aren't you paid to listen to me?' she asked with a sudden gesture of annoyance. 'I presume you're not here for a vacation.'

'No,' Simon replied. 'I'm not here for a vacation. I'm here to give you treatment. But I seem to have irritated you, and that's not how I deal with my patients. I do all I can *not* to annoy them.

Would you rather I left?'

'No,' Caroline answered. 'Unless you find my behaviour impossible to bear. And I do apologize.' Caroline was silent. The expression on her face was genuinely contrite. Simon was surprised at her illogical change of attitude. 'But you see,' she continued, 'for a long time I've lived up here alone in this apartment. I now realize that you must be the psychiatrist that my mother has been nattering about for the last fortnight. So I'd rather you did what you've been paid to do. In any case I'm enjoying having company for a change. So please don't go.'

She had become quite upset. Simon touched her gently on the arm in an attempt to calm her.

'Don't you dare touch me!' Caroline cried out suddenly. 'I can't bear being touched.' She turned away from him.

'May I ask why?' Simon enquired. 'What has made you afraid of being touched?'

Caroline was silent. Simon waited and sipped his drink.

'I'm afraid,' she whispered.

'What of?'

She glanced up at him. 'Those cuts and bruises on your face, they told me you were in the earthquake.' Simon nodded.

'That's a bit what it feels like, I think.'

'What exactly?' he asked, thinking he had slipped into the role of a psychiatrist quite easily.

She gave an odd little laugh. 'No, you're not a bit like the other psychiatrists. They were all so grave and earnest. You seem . . . so ordinary, in a way.' She paused, he waited, as he thought real psychiatrists must do. The silence went on. Caroline scanned the garden, narrowing her eyes, as if she had forgotten he was there, then she asked casually 'They've shown you to your room?'

'Yes.'

'They've given you the main guest room, I suppose? I had that, before I moved over here. I wonder if that room will do it to you?'

'Do what?'

'Don't you see how this apartment of mine is simple and clean? I insisted on that. I can't bear all that Moorish and Islamic design that makes one go mad, that's what it was doing to me. Some

39

mornings I seemed to enter into the design. I mean that, literally. I'd enter those coils and whorls and feel part of it, my whole body would circle around a labyrinth, a tangle of snakes. Those wrought iron shutters . . .' she shivered.

A vague recollection of Huxley and mescalin returned to him, something was there about becoming part of the furnishings – the folds in the curtains. 'Was it just the design?' he asked.

'Yes, I think so. But here, sometimes in the mornings when I'm staring out at the garden, I can feel part of a leaf, a flower, then enter its central stem. I quite like that. No, that doesn't frighten me. But other times . . . that's what I meant about the earthquake, the rooms here seem to move, swivel around, I feel they might crush me . . . I haven't told anyone about this. You don't think it's mad?' She turned to him. 'Tell me honestly.'

He shook his head.

'Why not?' she asked sharply.

He had reacted instinctively. Now she wanted a reason, he found it difficult to explain. 'If you were . . . well, unbalanced, I don't think you could be as objective about this as you are.'

Her face looked grim. 'Thank you,' she said. 'Because I think someone is drugging me. Someone here. I wouldn't put it past my own mother, except it doesn't help her for me to appear mad, so it can't be her. . . .'

'Do you hate her?'

'I loathe her,' Caroline said with cool disdain. 'Do you want to hear a little story, I mean that's why you're here, isn't it? So you might as well earn your fee.' She paused, then continued.

'When I was 9 there was a young coloured man-servant who worked in the house in Connecticut. He was about 19, tall and well-built and very strong. I suppose I admired him because I was young and had no colour prejudices. And he was wonderfully kind to me. His name was Joshua. He was one of the most beautiful people I'd ever seen. He always seemed to have some new toy that he had made for me or some idea for a picnic where he could drive me and my governess out into the country. He was my hero was Joshua. Remember I was only nine. But Joshua would never touch me – and I always longed to feel his smooth brown arms. I

40

really did love him.

'Betty ruined all that. One day I was playing in Betty's bedroom. I loved the smell and the feel of her dresses. I adored to paint and powder my face and to use my mother's expensive perfumes. That afternoon when I was in her bedroom I heard someone coming. I knew that my mother didn't really like me in her room – particularly if I had used some of her scent or make-up. If she found me in her bedroom she'd give me a real scolding. So when I heard someone approaching, I hid amongst the dresses in the wardrobe. I could pull the doors of the wardrobe almost together, but there was a gap which allowed me to see out into the bedroom and into a vast dressing-mirror. It was Betty who had disturbed me. She crossed over to the dressing-table and put on some scent. At that moment the door to her bedroom opened, and Joshua, my beloved man-servant, came in. She smiled and gestured for him to shut the door. She walked over and closed the curtains. Then Betty went up to Joshua. For a moment they stared at each other in silence. Then she took his head in her hands and kissed him fully on the mouth. "We can't stay long," my mother whispered to him, "so I'll do it the way you like most." He smiled at her. He didn't look like my Joshua any more. There was an arrogance in his face I had never seen. He stood there motionless as my mother undid his belt and pulled down the zip of his trousers. Reflected in that vast mirror I could see it all happening. I could not tear my eyes away from every gross thing she did to him as she knelt there at his feet. I could see each movement of her hands and her mouth. And I saw the expression – half-triumphant, half-disdainful – on Joshua's face as he looked down on her.'

Caroline got up from her chair and gazed out at the garden with its magnolia trees, bougainvillea and hibiscus.

'Have you always told this story to the doctors you have seen?' Simon asked gently.

'Oh yes, but I warn you my mother denies to all the doctors that she ever had a negro servant called Joshua. So if you mention it to her, you're bound to get the usual reaction.' She turned and leaned back on the balustrade. 'It's really quite funny. You see, there she is longing to prove me sane and normal, then she has to deny the truth and make out that I do suffer from delusions. Poor mother, she's in rather a spot and you're the one she's counting on.'

He stared past her towards the garden, the scent from a datura tree with its cream and yellow pendulous blossoms filled the air. 'Look, how long has this bitter relationship with your mother gone on?'

Caroline laughed. 'Oh, you really want to hear my story, do you? Only to have my version denied by her. Maybe the doctors who are coming should certify my mother?' She smiled and shrugged. 'It's what you'd call a classic Oedipal complex. Because I adored my father, and loved him beyond anything, I ran to him and told him what I had seen, well in a garbled kind of way, I suppose. I recall being sick and screaming. I thought my mother had turned into a cannibal you see. It wasn't the sex. It was the fact that she was eating one of our black servants. I suppose that's what I told my father. Well, I can't quite remember, it was all so confused. But she denied it, she plugged that her own mother had finished up in a bin. She said I was suffering from adolescent sexual delusions, got a doctor to agree and that's how it all began. My father was such a fool – Betty is very strong you know – she ruled him completely, yet he loved me too. Hence, the Will.' She paused. 'That's not all, something else happened too, but later. . . .'

'What?'

She smiled. 'I don't think I can tell you that, yet.'

He looked at her and saw how young and vulnerable she was; he felt a rush of tenderness overwhelm him.

Caroline had sat down again. 'Something very horrible happens every night here. That's what I'm now going to tell you.'

He leaned towards her, there seemed to be no problem about this patient not talking.

'Late – almost every night when I've gone to bed – a young Moroccan girl dressed in a white robe appears on this balcony. There is nothing so odd about that. But when she reaches the French windows of my bedroom, she begins to tap. Very gently, very gently — almost scratching at the glass. When I put on the lights and move towards the windows, she pulls open her robe and shows her naked body to me. Then she turns. Down her back are bleeding ridges — as if she had recently been savagely flogged. But always, always, always, by the time I get to the balcony, the girl has disappeared. There is no trace of her on the balcony. Not even a drop of blood.'

'How long is it since this girl first appeared?' Simon asked.

'A week after I moved into this part of the villa 6 months ago,' Caroline replied.

Simon went and looked over the balcony. The bougainvillea and trellis-work would make it an easy climb. The distance from the ground was slight — not even a dangerous jump. But why should the young girl appear? Who had flogged her? Why was it Caroline's balcony on which she appeared? Was it possible that the apparition was really a hallucination on Caroline's part?

'Do you hear any sound after she has disappeared?'

'No,' Caroline answered. 'The only noise I hear is when she is tapping on the window.'

'Has it occurred to you that the young Moroccan girl may be perfectly real?'

Caroline's glass was quivering in her hand. She put it down on the table. 'Of course it has,' she answered. 'Every night I try to persuade myself that she is real and I'm not suffering from any hallucinations. But she makes no sound — except for the quiet tapping. And, as I've told you, each evening by the time I've got out onto the balcony she's vanished. And how can the girl get into the compound? The walls are high, and there's a watchman at the gate.'

'Have you told your mother about this?' Simon asked.

'I did when the girl first appeared,' Caroline answered. I thought she was real, and I thought she might have some accomplice who was going to break into the house and burgle it. I don't know exactly what I thought. But I felt it was all very sinister. My mother told Toni and Sheila Adams. Toni questioned the night watchman, but he had neither seen nor heard anything. So when it happened again a few nights later my mother began to think it was one of my hallucinations.'

'Tell me about your mother's secretary, Sheila Adams.'

'To tell you the truth I don't awfully like her,' Caroline replied. 'But I do see that she's an essential part of the household. Because though Toni speaks fluent English, he can't read it very easily, and he's hopeless about dealing with bills and so on. So Sheila's useful because she's very competent.'

'What don't you like about her?' Simon asked. He wanted to gather as much information as he could about the people in the villa.

'The fact that she makes such a desperate effort to be an imitation of my mother – in her make-up, her clothes and her conversation,' Caroline answered. 'She even wears dresses that my mother has got bored with. I think she envies our style of living. People say that we all have a besetting sin. Well, her's is definitely envy.'

'How long has Sheila been with your mother?' Simon asked.

'We found her one evening in a café in Tangier. She was rather drunk, and she was having drinks with a hideous Moroccan of about 50 who was obviously sponging on her because Sheila was paying for all the drinks. She was very heavily made-up. Her forced gaiety was painful to watch. But for some reason mother took to her. Perhaps she was sorry for her. Perhaps she sensed that Sheila could be very useful. Anyhow she took her on, and eventually the woman came to live here in this villa. I don't really mind her. At least she tries to make herself useful. For instance our cook, our Fatima, can't make the electric juice extractor work to make my orange juice. Sheila goes into the kitchen and copes with it and supervizes the food we're going to eat. But Sheila is in no way a prisoner. One evening a week Toni drives her into Casablanca. Toni goes to the bars to meet his old friends, and he maintains that Sheila goes to the cinema. But I think once she's got rid of Toni she goes to some bar where she can pick up a Moroccan – and heaven knows what they then do together. But at least Sheila doesn't fuss over me as mother does. I do object to being treated as if I were some valuable piece of porcelain. Perhaps I should confess something to you – because

44

I'm almost beginning to think of you as a friend to whom I can confess my errors. . . . My mother isn't as well off as she was, and she has, after all, paid out a lot of money on my doctors' fees and everything so I promised her all on my own accord to let her have a third of what I get from the trust – if indeed I get a single penny. So mother's determined that I must pass my examination with the doctors. And that's where you come in. And who knows? Perhaps you and this new drug will do the trick.'

Caroline got up from her chair and moved towards him. 'I like being with you,' she said. 'You have a calming presence.' Then she smiled. 'But I must confess there is another reason why I like you; it's because you let me do most of the talking.'

As Caroline stood gazing at him with a smile on her face Simon decided that with her wide-set hazel eyes, snub nose and broad mouth her face was enchanting and the shape of her slim body with her small, firm breasts and fragile waist thrilled him.

'I shan't be coming over to dinner tonight,' Caroline told him. 'But please will you visit me tomorrow morning – any time after 10 o'clock.'

'I shall look forward to it,' Simon answered. 'But before I go let me assure you that in my own opinion you are not only perfectly sane, but also legally competent. I can't understand what all the anxiety has been about.'

She threw back her head and laughed. 'Well, *I* think I'm legally competent of course.' She hesitated. 'Also,' she added quietly, 'I think I'm sane. I know what others call my hallucinations are real.'

'That's what I intend to prove,' Simon said. He went to the door. 'I'll see you tomorrow then.'

Chapter 6

The sun had lost its brilliance as Simon sat down by the pool; a banana tree with its frilled green leaves was silhouetted against the sky. He watched a trail of black ants carrying balls of red earth to and fro from the flower bed; to him, their strenuous activity seemed pointless. Some ants carried the earth to a crack in the paving stones, while other ants carried the earth back again to the flower bed. Like military detention, he thought: with pick axes we broke down a brick wall and the next week we built it up again. But the ants must know what they're doing. And someone, he didn't know who, someone in this house knew what they were doing with Caroline and the inheritance. There was so much that did not add up. It was as if he had heard only a fragment of the plot that Caroline was enmeshed in. Could Betty fill in other details?

He returned to his room and showered. His suitcases had been unpacked and he now dressed himself with care, enjoying the feel of the cream linen suit he had bought that morning.

'Help yourself to a drink,' Betty said as he came into the long white living-room. She was wearing a red dress of some shimmering material that fitted her too closely. There was a glass in her hand.

'I drink vodka at this time of night,' she added. 'But help yourself to whatever you want.' Simon poured himself a small whisky.

'How did your interview go?' Betty asked him.

'Fine,' Simon answered. 'I can assure you of one thing. Your daughter is not mad. Nervous and highly strung certainly. But perfectly sane. And there should be no question of her legal competence being proved.'

'Did you give her any of your medicine?' she asked.

'No,' Simon replied. 'But I will tomorrow.'

'Did she tell you about her hallucination of a girl on the balcony?'

'Yes,' Simon answered. 'If you don't mind I'll reserve my opinion on that matter for the time being.'

'Remember you haven't got long.'

'I've got as long as I need,' Simon replied.

Betty took a gulp of her drink. 'Did Caroline talk about money?' she asked. 'Did she speak about her inheritance?'

Simon had an instinct that he must lie. 'No,' he answered.

'I only wondered,' Betty continued. 'One of her hallucinations is that I made her promise that she would give me a third of the money if she is declared sane. Of course I did nothing of the sort. Why should I? After all, I'm perfectly well off as it is. But I thought I should warn you of that particular hallucination.'

'Thank you,' Simon said. 'It may prove most helpful.' Already he had begun to find that part of him was indeed a psychiatrist. Perhaps with some training a new job in life lay ahead of him. Then he laughed at himself because of his fantasy. He must wait for the right opportunity to leave the house, and yet he was unwilling to leave Caroline in her present state. Someone might be trying to haunt her, and perhaps was succeeding.

Betty glanced at the gold watch on her wrist. 'I can't imagine where Toni can be,' she said. 'He knows I like him to be down here at this hour. The intercom in his room doesn't answer. But sometimes when he wants to have a sleep in the afternoon he switches it off.'

'Toni had an exhausting day collecting me,' Simon murmured. He glanced at Betty, then continued. 'Your daughter also told me about Joshua.'

Betty nodded and slowly took a long sip from her glass. 'The little brat has a filthy mind. She tried to come between me and Henry. I adored that man. But,' she sighed, 'I do think these fantasies of hers were just a part of adolescence. That's what all the doctors told me.' She turned to Simon. 'You don't believe Caroline, I hope? We never had a negro servant called Joshua. We

47

never had a negro servant in Connecticut at all.'

Simon murmured assent as Betty pushed over a silver bowl of nuts. She shoved them rather too harshly, he thought, for they almost fell off the glass table.

'Caroline was riddled with jealousy in those years. Talk about a tortured adolescent! But lately I've been feeling that she's getting over it – that she and I can have a real affectionate relationship. Whatever she's done in the past, I'm willing to forget it.'

'That's generous of you.' Simon sipped his whisky and examined her closely. There was something heavily sensual, almost gross, about her features. He could not quite see her as a loyal and faithful wife.

'Did she tell you the other vile thing that I'm supposed to have done?'

Simon recalled that Caroline had said there was something else. He shook his head.

'Oh, she'll get around to it. So you'd better hear it from me first.' Betty got up and poured herself another vodka. If she wasn't a liar, Betty certainly seemed to be an alcoholic, he thought.

'According to Caroline I seduced my own step-son, yes Clifton,' she said. 'That was the summer of fifty-three. We had a wild hectic love affair, in Caroline's version. So she spilt the beans to Henry about that too.'

'How did she find out?'

'Find out what?' Betty asked sharply. 'There was nothing to find out. She made it all up. He came down once to that house to beg me for money to buy his damned drugs. He even stayed a night, I think. But that was enough for Caroline; she was 14 at the time. Again, the doctors told me it was a fantasy that adolescent girls are prone to have.'

Simon nodded. 'I see,' he murmured. What was the truth he wondered? Betty's manner made him feel that it was fantasy, but when he had been with Caroline, he had believed her completely.

Betty had sat down next to him again. 'You see how urgent it is that none of these stories get out to the doctors when they see her. She must be tranquillized, yet not appear to be so. She has days when she is quite calm. In a way it's good that she comes out with all this crap to you. Maybe she'll work it out of her system.' Betty glanced again at her watch. 'Where the hell can Toni be? If you'll excuse me, I'll go and look for him.'

Simon rose as she left the room. He was feeling slightly drunk. He must be careful, he thought. He crammed a handful of nuts into his mouth, chewed them and stared about the room. On the side table there was a silver framed photograph; it was a wedding picture of Betty and a man who was obviously Henry. Simon picked it up. Betty was laughing into the camera, her large painted mouth open; she looked a little vulgar – as if she was imitating a Hollywood star of that period; her hair was peroxide white like Harlow; Henry in his morning suit looked sensitive and shy. It was a strange contrast. He could see that Caroline took after Henry, for he had the brash, clean, gusto of an American college boy – a wide grin and freckles – but he also looked nervous, as if not quite certain what he had landed himself with. Simon replaced the photograph and sat down again on the sofa.

He considered Betty's attitude to her daughter. On one hand she smothered her with care and affection, taking immense trouble over her daughter's mental stability and health, so that Caroline would inherit her father's wealth; yet also, she resented and even disliked her daughter. If Betty had told the truth, she even had good reason for disliking her; if Betty were lying, she had more reason to dislike her. Exactly, he thought, it didn't add up. Wouldn't Betty want to take her revenge upon her daughter, allow her to seem insane on her 21st birthday, and so disinherit her? Yet perhaps one-third of the inheritance was worth more to her than revenge?

He looked up and noticed that a Moroccan of about 50 had glided soundlessly into the room. The man inclined his head. 'Dr Orville,' he murmured, 'I'm Azziz, head servant to Mrs Morrison. Dinner is served.' He half turned and Simon rose and followed him.

There was a strained atmosphere at dinner. The food and the wine were excellent, but Betty kept staring with her protuberant eyes at the empty chair on her left. Simon sat on her right; Sheila sat at the end of the table facing Betty; her thick layer of lipstick left a mark on her wine glass. She answered Betty's question civilly and listened to the stories which Betty insisted on telling of the celebrities she had known when she lived in London, but Simon had an impression that Sheila was hostile to both Betty and himself, and he wondered why.

Betty was in the middle of one of her stories about the stars and celebrities in the film world. 'Then Noël turned to Tallulah,' she told them, 'and said to her, "This dry martini is as tepid as you are over-heated. I think you could both do with some ice."'

'He is a witty man,' Sheila said.

'But you've never even met him,' Betty told her.

'I can still read his plays and books,' Sheila answered.

At that moment Toni walked in.

'Where in heaven's name have you been?' Betty asked him.

Toni sat down at the table. 'Let me explain,' he said. 'I'm late because I heard a rumour of a piece of news, so I wanted to make sure it was true.'

'What news?' Betty asked.

'Clifton Morrison has arrived in Casablanca,' Toni declared. 'He's been in the country for some time. He is living in a small house owned by a Moroccan friend of his.'

'You're certain?' Betty asked.

'I made absolutely certain. I even had a chat with one of the servants from the house,' Toni replied. 'That's why I'm late. I thought you'd want to know.'

'Indeed, I'd want to know,' Betty stated. 'And I'm most interested. I always thought to myself that Clifton would want to be somewhere near us on the crucial day. But I'm sure that you, Toni, and Dr Orville will see to it that my darling Caroline is not bothered by him. Besides, if it comes to force we have four male servants who would have no difficulty in turning him out of the house. Indeed, I think it's far better that Caroline should not know of his arrival at all. They never did get on well together.'

'I'm sure that there is no reason to worry,' Toni said. 'But I thought we ought to be on our guard.'

'Quite right,' Betty said. 'And you'd better alert the servants. But now let's drink to celebrate the fact that Dr Orville is convinced that Caroline is quite competent legally, and will be proved to be so on her birthday.'

Dutifully they raised their glasses. Then Betty added: 'He seems to think Caroline is sane, as well.' There was an edge of sourness in her voice which worried Simon.

Simon drank to the toast and thought the strange thing was that he did feel convinced Caroline was quite sane, but he was no psychiatrist, and supposing he was wrong. . . ? Yet Betty needed him here; besides he felt drawn to Caroline; he had a strong feeling that he wanted to help this lonely girl, also he now wanted to discover the truth.

Betty continued with more theatrical stories about celebrities in New York. She had obviously financed several successful productions with her husband's money. The palatial splendour of this villa did not indicate that she was at all short of cash, yet people still lived in style when they were almost in debt. He glanced at Sheila, there was something triumphant, a little smug about her manner. Then he remembered that when Toni had entered with his news, she had dropped her fork. She had seemed more surprised than Betty. In fact, Betty had shown no surprise at all. If Betty 7 years ago had played the role of Phaedra, could she still be obsessed with her stepson? Together were they planning to disinherit Caroline? But if so, why bring Dr Orville from Geneva?

'I'm sorry, will you excuse me? I must have a good night's sleep,' Simon addressed himself to Betty. 'It's been a long day and I want to spend a lot of time with Caroline tomorrow.'

Betty dabbed her lips with a napkin. 'Dr Orville, I'm so grateful to you.' She extended her plump hand, he held it for a moment. It was very hot and he saw in her eyes an anxiety she did not express.

Chapter 7

When Simon reached his room he did not take off his clothes. He walked on to his balcony and looked out into the garden. There was no one about. Presumably the watchman was in his small hut at the main gate. The lights were still on in Caroline's rooms. Simon went back into his room and turned out all the lights. He placed a bamboo chair in a position on the balcony from which he couldn't be seen from the garden below. Once again, he wondered whether his belief that Caroline was quite sane might be false, yet for some reason he was convinced that the girl was normal, for all her nervousness. He was perplexed by the strange visitations of the Arab girl, and he was determined to find out the truth of the matter. He settled down to wait.

Presently the lights in Caroline's apartment were extinguished. The moon was partly obscured by clouds, but the night was not dark, and he could see Caroline's balcony quite clearly. He passed the time by wondering who could have instructed the little Moroccan girl, for he was almost certain that she was not a hallucination of Caroline's. If he could prove that the girl was real it would help Caroline greatly, and by doing so he would relieve his own feelings of guilt which still persisted. Then he heard a faint noise. A few moments later he saw a figure in white climb on to the far side of Caroline's balcony. The figure was very slim, and it moved towards one of the windows and began tapping gently on the glass. The lights were switched on in Caroline's apartment. The tapping continued. The light was now bright on the balcony so Caroline must have drawn back her curtains. He could see the figure plainly. It was a young girl in a white robe. She was unveiled. At that moment she opened her robe and pulled it aside so that her back was revealed. An instant later she vanished over the far side of the balcony. He could see a gleam of white among the mimosa bushes; then it disappeared.

Quickly Simon left his room and made his way to Caroline's apartment. In the silence of the night he could hear Caroline sobbing convulsively. He tried to open the door, but it was locked.

'Caroline,' he called out quietly. 'I must see you.'

'Go away,' her muffled voice said. 'Leave me alone.'

'Caroline, please,' Simon said. 'It's really important.'

'It can wait till morning,' her voice answered. 'I'll see you to-morrow.'

Simon went back to his room, undressed and got into bed. But he could not sleep. In his mind he could still hear the sound of Caroline crying. He was perturbed that he had become so concerned about her. It did not fit in with his plans.

The following morning there was a knock on Simon's door, and Azziz appeared with coffee and croissants. After breakfast Simon dressed and collected from his suitcase the mild sleeping tablets which he had taken in hospital when he couldn't sleep. He held the bottle under the hot tap in the bathroom and took off the label. The tablets were not marked. He knew he must pretend they were his 'wonder drug' as Betty insisted on calling it. If Caroline took one in the morning and one in the evening the only effect would be to make her feel drowsy. He put the bottle in his pocket and went downstairs. There was no one about. Simon opened the front door and wandered out. The crenellated wall ran all the way around the garden, but he saw again that on the other side of the compound there was a small door shaped like a keyhole fixed in the wall. He tried to open it, but it was locked. He turned and climbed the steps which led to Caroline's rooms. He knocked at the door. There was no reply. 'Caroline', he called out.

'Who is it?' Caroline answered from inside.

For a moment he was about to say 'Simon'; then he remembered. 'Orville,' he said.

He heard the sound of a key turning in the lock, and the door opened. Caroline was wearing white trousers and a short linen coat.

53

'Good morning,' Simon said.

For a while Caroline stared at him in silence. 'Have you come to this villa to spy on me?' she asked.

'No,' Simon answered. 'But why should you think so?'

'I had one of my attacks last night,' Caroline told him. 'For a moment I had a hallucination. I suppose I must have broken down. But the next thing I knew you were knocking on my door. You must have been listening outside.'

'No,' Simon said. 'I came up your stairs because I heard you crying and I wondered if you were all right. What's more I had something important to tell you.'

'What was the important thing?'

'Let's sit down.'

Caroline hesitated, then moved towards an orange-coloured sofa at the end of the room. Simon followed her and sat down next to her.

'What I have to say is very simple but very important,' he said. 'The girl you see on your balcony is real. You don't have any hallucination at all. From my bedroom I can see your balcony. With my own eyes I saw the girl appear on it. That's why I hurried round to your room. I wanted to tell you that you were not imagining the Arab girl. I don't know how she gets into the garden – unless it's through the little door at the back. But she's definitely a real person.'

Caroline's hazel eyes were gazing at him. 'I wish I could believe you,' she said.

'I've told you the truth,' Simon replied. 'Why should I lie to you?'

'Because you want to get me in a fit state to be examined by the two doctors in a few days.'

'The Moroccan girl is real,' Simon repeated.

'Why can't you be honest with me?' Caroline cried out. 'Why do you have to keep pretending? I may be mad, but at least I can tell a lie when I hear one. And what about those tablets of yours which are supposed to contain a "wonder drug"? I haven't even heard you mention them.'

'Well, you will hear me mention them now,' Simon said.

54

He crossed over to the drink table, took out his bottle of tablets and put one in a small glass. Then he poured some orange juice into a tumbler and went back to Caroline.

'I want you to take this tablet now,' he said. 'They will make you feel a little sleepy.' He put the glass containing the tablet and the tumbler of orange juice on a small table close to Caroline.

Caroline was watching him carefully. 'How do I know that you haven't been bribed by someone?' she asked. 'How do I know that the tablet doesn't contain poison?'

'You don't,' Simon replied. 'But if you like, I'll take one of the tablets myself.'

Caroline was silent. Simon walked over to the drink table, took one of the tablets from the bottle, poured out a little orange juice, turned around to Caroline, showed her the tablet, put it in his mouth and swallowed it with the orange juice. He laughed. 'Now do you believe me?' he enquired.

Suddenly Caroline began to cry. 'Why can't I trust anyone?' she asked. 'Why do I feel that everyone is conspiring against me?'

Simon sat down on the sofa beside her. 'I can't tell you the answer to that question as yet,' he said quietly. 'But I can tell you this in all honesty: I want to help you. And I will. Would you have confidence in me if I caught the Moroccan girl when she next appears? Would you have confidence in me if I were to catch the girl as she climbed down from your balcony?'

Caroline was staring at him. 'Yes,' she whispered. 'I'm sure I would.'

Without thinking he took her hand. 'Whatever happens,' he said, 'whatever happens I want you to believe that I'm going to do everything I can to help you. And I'm certain I *can* help you. . . . Caroline,' he continued, 'the important thing is that you should believe me when I say that I've become fond of you. But I think you do believe it — because I'm still holding your hand, and you haven't tried to move away from me, and you've stopped crying.'

'Yes,' Caroline said quietly, 'I think I do trust you.' Gently Caroline removed her hand from his, raised the glass, and swallowed the tablet with some orange juice. Then she smiled at him.

'Now let me hold your hand again,' he said.

She stretched her arm across the divan. He held her hand. For a while there was silence. As he looked into her eyes Simon realized with a shock that he was extremely attracted by her. He wondered if Caroline would guess the fact; he was afraid that she would retire into her shell of self-contemplation if she did discover the truth about him.

Then Caroline spoke. 'I told you that I hated being touched. But with you I find it different. You have given me a sense of security – more than any of the other doctors have done. . . . Do you realize that I don't even know your Christian name?'

For a second Simon hesitated. 'Paul,' he replied.

'Why did you hesitate just now?'

'I can't imagine.'

He held her hand tighter, then released it. 'Caroline, you said yesterday, there was something else, something more awful, than Joshua. . . .'

She threw back her head and smiled at him. 'I forget. I only remembered this morning, but did you mention Joshua to Mother?' Simon nodded. 'And she denied that he ever existed?'

'True.'

Caroline had gone to a book-case and she drew out a slim volume of poetry. It was worn, and its binding was discoloured. *The Hunting of the Snark* – I loved it when I was small, I still do. I always kept my favourite photographs in it. But you see all the other photographs and snaps disappeared when I was young, but I found this one only the other week.' She took it from the book and handed it to Simon. It was of a girl with pigtails sitting astride a pony. Holding the reins was a young, handsome negro. 'Turn it over,' Caroline said. 'Katy was my pony.' Simon saw that in a round childish handwriting there was an inscription: 'Me, Katy and Joshua.'

'That's interesting,' Simon murmured. 'I wonder whether we ought to show it to your mother to prove that he did exist?'

'Or to a psychiatrist like you?' Caroline said, sitting down next to him.

He handed the snap back to her. 'Keep it for now, we may

need it. Now, you see we are making progress. Two of what they called your hallucinations have been proved to be real.

'Did you doubt me?' she asked. There was a tremor in her voice.

He squeezed her hand again. 'No, I didn't. But this other thing, can't you tell me about that?'

'Has she told you?'

'Yes, she mentioned it and denied it. She claimed it was one of your adolescent fantasies.'

Caroline put her feet up on a stool and lay her head back on a cushion. She spoke quietly. 'It was one of those long hot summers like when all those Southern writers make adolescent girls have their sexual fantasies, except I think it was Betty having one. Father had to stay in New York. There was a lake in the grounds of our new house and one morning I saw this empty boat just drifting without anyone. It was our rowing boat, generally tied up against an old wooden jetty, but it was floating and I watched. I walked round the lake, and gradually the boat came in and stopped, held by some weeds and rushes near the shore. When I got there, it wasn't empty, Clifton was lying naked, half asleep or stoned, I don't know. He was the first man I saw really naked.' She paused. 'We talked. He said he'd come down late in the night and was staying. He just drifted around for the next few days doing his own thing. He seemed to stay up all night and sleep until about noon. But he would eat with us in the evenings and I just knew by the way Betty looked at him, I just knew what she wanted.'

'Is that your only proof?'

'No, that's not all. But the look of hunger, it's unmistakable. Clifton would disappear for a few days and then I could see Betty going mad, fretting and pacing the room. I think Clifton went off and bought drugs, because when he came back he was different, kind of all of one piece, quite charming, but always a bit cynical towards her. I think she was paying, giving him the money for the drugs, and he wasn't giving her what she wanted. She knew she wouldn't get him unless she stopped the drugs, stopped the flow of cash and destroyed what he had already bought. Well, that's the gist of what I overheard one night.' Caroline turned and stared at Simon. 'There was an almighty row which woke me. I got up and went out of my room. Clifton was screaming at her, he broke a mirror in her bedroom, I heard the crash, but she was quite calm. I heard her say, yes, she would give him the drugs, if he shared her bed and then. . . .'

'What?'

'I was outside the bedroom. I heard Clifton sobbing and her voice soothing him, as if he was a baby. There were no more rows that summer. I knew from Betty's expression she was no longer hungry, and I knew, from remarks Clifton made, how much he despised her.'

'You never saw them together?'

'No'.

'So what happened then?'

'Nothing. I know she says that I went and told father, but that's untrue. Clifton disappeared one day and she stayed in her room, said she was ill. Maybe she guessed that I knew the truth. Because she got a doctor to examine me soon afterwards and I told him. Only because he kept on asking me questions about that summer and Clifton. Mother must have been terrified that I knew the truth and would tell father, so she got this doctor to examine me who would prove that my idea about Clifton was a hallucination.'

'I wonder . . . .' Simon paused. 'D'you think she still hears from him?'

Caroline shrugged. 'It's Toni she's mad about now. I think she must hate Clifton.'

'You sound tired. Perhaps we should stop for today?'

Caroline got up from the sofa. 'I'm feeling a bit sleepy. I suppose it's your tablet working.'

'I doubt that,' Simon said. 'But you did have a disturbed night.'

'Anyway, will you come back at 6 o'clock this evening for a drink?' Caroline asked.

Simon got up and went to her and put his hands on her shoulders. 'I'll see you at six,' he said. Then he leaned forward and kissed her on the forehead.

For a moment Caroline was motionless. 'Please remember I've never known a man at all well,' she murmured. 'so please don't seem surprised that I'm a bit confused. I can only tell you that I like you. I like you very much.'

Chapter 8

When Simon went downstairs to lunch he found Sheila alone in the living-room.

'Betty has driven into Casablanca with Toni,' she informed him. 'So the two of us are alone. I hope you don't mind?'

Simon could not understand the hostility in her voice. 'Of course I don't mind,' Simon replied.

There was a pause. 'Would you like me to pour you a drink?' Sheila asked. 'I've made a dry martini.'

'I'd love one,' Simon replied.

Sheila moved towards the drink cabinet. 'Please don't bother,' Simon said. 'I'll help myself.'

'Don't worry,' Sheila said, pouring out the drink 'When Toni's not about I'm supposed to act as barman . . . . Tell me – as a psychiatrist do you approve of drink?' she asked.

'As a psychiatrist,' Simon replied, 'I approve with reservations. As a private individual – I'm afraid I approve 100 per cent.'

'Where did you study psychiatry?' Sheila asked.

'At Cambridge,' Simon replied. 'And then in London.'

'At one of the big hospitals?' Sheila asked.

This was the kind of question Simon had been dreading. 'No,' he answered. 'I studied at a psychiatric clinic.'

Sheila began twisting a silver ring on her little finger. For some reason she seemed to Simon to be very tense. Azziz came in to say that lunch was ready. In silence they walked into the dining-room.

'I've ordered you a light meal,' Sheila told him, 'as I didn't think you would want to eat a lot in the middle of the day. But if you'd like anything more I'll summon Azziz, and he'll go and tell the Fatima. The two servants who will wait on us at lunch speak a little French but no English, so we needn't be careful what we say.'

A young Moroccan servant came in and handed to each of them in turn a dish of brochettes on skewers. Another servant followed him carrying vegetables on a large platter.

'How do you find Caroline?' Sheila asked when they began eating.

'As you know, I told Betty that in my opinion Caroline is highly strung but perfectly sane.'

'Is it sane to have hallucinations?' Sheila asked.

Immediately, Simon saw a trap. He no longer trusted Sheila. 'So far as I'm concerned she has only got one hallucination in particular,' he stated. 'And I'm sure you know about it. But not one of us is perfectly sane. The borderline between sanity and insanity is sometimes very thin.'

'We may all be a little insane, but we don't look out of our window and see a Moroccan girl with the marks of a whip on her back,' Sheila remarked.

Some instinct told Simon not to let her know his conviction that the Moroccan girl was a reality. 'That's a problem that may be resolved by investigation,' Simon answered.

'Has the medicine had any effect so far?' Sheila asked.

'Yes,' he suppressed a yawn; it had certainly had an effect on him.

'How do you administer it, Dr Orville? By injection or in pill form?'

'In Caroline's case I've given her tablets to take.'

'Which contain your "wonder drug" I presume?'

'Yes, but I don't call them "wonder drugs" myself.'

'But your patients do,' Sheila stated. 'Betty was most impressed by what she heard from a friend of hers who had been to see you in Geneva.'

'I'm glad to hear it.'

'What was her name?' Sheila asked, frowning, as if she had had a sudden lapse of memory.

There was a pause, while Simon stabbed a piece of pork with

his fork and placed it into his mouth.

Sheila clicked her fingers. 'I really ought to remember, she writes to Betty about everyone and really . . . she's one of Betty's old friends.' Sheila stared at him enquiringly.

The piece of pork remained in his mouth, he chewed it and yet he couldn't swallow it. Then he heard himself saying: 'I never discuss my patients with anyone.'

Sheila smiled. They went on eating in silence for a moment.

'But when we heard that you had been in the earthquake we were, of course, afraid for your sake, and naturally we were concerned about the medicine. We thought it might have been destroyed.

'No,' Simon answered without hesitation. 'It had been very carefully packed in my despatch case which was recovered from the rubble of the Hotel Saada.'

By now Simon was convinced that Sheila believed that he was an imposter and was trying to corner him.

'But surely you haven't allowed much time for the drug to work?' Sheila said. 'Remember the doctors are coming in only a few days time.'

'The tablets have an immediate effect,' Simon told her.

'But I presume they don't have the same effect on every single one of your patients?'

'I can only assure you that they are having a good effect on Caroline.'

'And have they removed her hallucinations?'

'Partly,' Simon answered.

'You mean you've persuaded her not to say anything about the Moroccan girl to the doctors?'

'No,' Simon answered. 'I'm here to cure Caroline – not to hoodwink two specialists from New York.'

The servants cleared away their plates and brought in large bowls of salad.

'Does Caroline know that her half-brother Clifton is in Casablanca?' Sheila asked.

'No,' Simon answered. 'And I don't intend she *should* know.'

'So you still don't consider her as a very stable patient?'

Simon could feel anger filling him as he looked at the thick make-up on Sheila's face, but he forced his voice to sound calm. 'I've told you that I believe Caroline to be legally competent,' he said. 'That is the question which the doctors will have to decide upon. Not her nervous stability.'

'Speaking of stability,' Sheila said, 'Betty is very worried about Clifton arriving. That's why she asked Toni to drive her into Casablanca. She's gone to see a Moroccan friend of hers who's high up in the police. She is going to ask him to keep an eye on Clifton.'

'Have you ever met Clifton?'

'No. But I've heard he's not as black as Betty paints him.'

'Why do you think he has come to Casablanca?' Simon asked.

'I suppose it is because he wants the doctors' report to be accurate. He doesn't want any trickery. After all, he's got a lot to lose or gain. But that's only my own guesswork.' Sheila pushed back her chair. 'Will you excuse me if I don't stay for coffee?' she said. 'I've got some work to do before I take my siesta. If you want a liqueur, please help yourself. See you at dinner.'

'Thank you,' Simon answered. He rose from his chair as Sheila left the room.

The pill had affected him. He had needed to think, so he had returned to his room, lain on the bed and fallen asleep.

In his dream he was lying naked beneath the rubble; the noise of his rescuers could be heard faintly, yet the beam above him thrust down upon his chest, so that he was sinking further and further down into the debris. He knew he would be buried in the soft sand which would pour into his mouth. Then the rescuers shone torches and he could see the space he was trapped in. He twisted around, tried to stumble to his feet, then fell to his hands and knees. The floor was moving again, something beneath the floor was about to erupt to the surface. He stared at the quivering spot, terrified of whatever it was and then suddenly a skeletal hand jutted out and grasped his arm. He pulled away. He shouted: 'Help!' But as he pulled away the rest of the skeleton came to the surface and upon it there still clung remnants of rotting flesh. His lips moved – the skeleton's lips – he recognized Dr

Orville. The *real* Dr Orville.

'I'm rotting beneath the hotel,' he mumbled. 'For 10 days I was crushed but lying there still alive, rotting away, my body wracked with thirst, hunger, pain. Why didn't you tell them I was still there? Why did you murder me? Why did you take my name from me?'

The skeleton clung to him; he could smell the putrefaction, feel the rotting flesh, slimy and cold, rubbing against his naked body. 'Now I'm taking you with me, you'll die the same way. There'll be no rescue for you, not the second time.'

Simon woke up sweating and still quivering with fear. He threw his clothes into a corner and showered. 'Damn you, Orville,' he muttered, as the warm water washed away the last vestiges of sleep. 'You died instantaneously, I'm not having you haunting me.' He dried himself, lit a cigarette and went back to the bed. He glanced at his watch: he had an hour before he saw Caroline again, and he badly needed to think.

Sheila knew he was an imposter. How could she know? If she knew, did Betty know? Obviously if Sheila knew, it was likely that Betty had taken her into her confidence. Suppose Betty had gone into Casablanca that day to meet Clifton? This seemed likely and yet Betty's manner to him had always convinced Simon that she believed him to be Dr Orville. It was impossible. He was going round in circles. The only person who seemed to accept him happily and simply was Caroline, whom they all thought to be insane.

He stared at the intricately decorated room and remembered how it had disorientated Caroline. At this hour the perfumes from the garden entered the house making it seem even more exotic. He rose from the bed, wrapped in the towel, and went on to his balcony. The datura tree grew immediately beneath him. He stared at the long creamy golden blooms which exuded a strong scent of sweetened lemon and recalled a book he had read some years ago about Peru. The natives boiled these flowers and drank the liquid. It was a hallucinogenic drug; some of them, addicted to the visions that the brew gave, even died of it.

Sheila picked and arranged the flowers for the house.

64

Chapter 9

At 6 o'clock Simon knocked on the door of Caroline's apartment.

'Who is it?' Caroline called out.

'Paul,' he answered.

The door opened. Caroline was wearing a thick bath-robe. Bound round her waist was an ornate Moroccan belt. Immediately he saw her Simon realized that any hostility she had ever felt towards him had now been dispelled.

'Good evening, Paul,' she said, smiling at him. 'Please forgive me for not being more conventionally dressed. But that tablet you gave me put me to sleep. I've only just woken up, and I've just had time to take a bath. I never thought you'd be so punctual. But if you want me to dress I'll go into my bedroom and put on something or other.'

'No,' Simon said. 'I think you look splendid in the bath-robe. It suits you.'

Caroline looked at the turtle-neck sweater Simon was wearing. 'And I see,' she murmured, 'that you are less formally dressed than before.'

Simon smiled back at her. 'That's because this isn't a formal visit,' he said. 'I was invited to come and have a drink with you.'

'Good,' Caroline said. 'I've just made a champagne cocktail. Would you like one?'

'Fine,' Simon said.

'I like you in your sweater,' Caroline said as she handed him his drink. 'It makes you look far younger.'

Simon laughed. 'How old do you think I am?' he asked.

She looked him up and down. 'I like your figure,' she said.

'But not my face?'

'Yes, I like your face. All I meant to say was that somehow

your figure is younger than your face. But I would say that you were forty.'

'Let's leave it at that,' Simon said smiling. 'I'm 40, and you'll be 21 at the end of the week. Are you nervous?'

'Yes,' Caroline answered. 'But less nervous than I was before.'

'Why, may I ask?'

'I don't think it's because of the tablet I had,' Caroline answered. 'In fact I know what it is. But you'll probably laugh at me.'

'No,' Simon replied. 'I won't laugh at you.'

'Then I'll tell you the truth,' Caroline said. 'I know that I'll be less nervous at my examination because you'll be here in the villa. Whatever they decide, I know that I have got someone to rely upon. Promise me you won't leave the villa until the doctors have gone.'

'I promise. But you do realize that I will probably not be allowed to be present when they examine you? However, as I've already told you, I'm convinced that you're sane. And tonight, if the girl appears, I'll prove it to you.'

'How can you do that?'

'By waiting below your balcony and catching her when she comes down. If I can, I'll bring her up and show her to you.' Simon raised his glass. 'I'm drinking to the end of your hallucination,' he said.

'Who could be doing it?' Caroline asked. 'Who could have organized the Arab girl?'

'I don't know,' Simon answered. 'But I intend to find out.'

Caroline's face was solemn. She looked very fragile in her robe, and her eyes were clouded. The bath-robe was too large for her which made her look like a very young girl dressed in her mother's clothes.

'What happens then?' Caroline asked. 'What if they declare me legally competent? The doctors will give their opinion and go. And the next day I suppose you will fly back to Geneva, and I'll be alone again?'

'As Betty may have told you, I more or less retired when I inherited some money,' Simon said. 'I've no relations or close

66

friends. I'm as alone as you are. So I can promise you this. As long as you need me, I'll stay here.'

'You don't think I'm mad?' Caroline asked. 'I don't mean insane, I mean 'mad' to talk as I'm doing to you – when we've only known each other for such a short time.'

'I can assure you that if you're mad, then I'm mad too,' Simon answered.

There was silence. They were still standing watching each other.

'Come here,' Caroline said softly to him. Simon moved towards her. Caroline put her hands on his shoulders and gazed into his face. Then slowly she bent down his head and kissed him on the lips. Simon put his arm around her and held her to him. He could feel her breasts pressing against him.

Abruptly she broke away. He thought that at the last moment she had become afraid. But, without looking at him she crossed over to the door and locked it.

'Remember that I'm constantly spied on,' she said.

Suddenly Simon was nervous. Was her fear of being spied on a part of one of her hallucinations or was she genuinely afraid of the close watch that her mother kept over her?

Caroline came back and stood facing him. Simon took her head in his hands and kissed her on the lips. She put her arms around him and held him close to her.

'You know that I've never been with a man before, and it's true. Please be gentle with me.' She was trembling. 'I want you,' she said. 'But I'm frightened.'

'There's no need to be.'

He took hold of her hand and led her towards the door of the bedroom.

'I won't tell anyone,' she whispered. 'I promise you.'

'Has anyone ever told you how beautiful you are?'

'A young doctor once made a pass at me,' she told him. 'I wouldn't even let him touch me. But with you it's different because I want you.'

'You're sure you won't regret it?'.

'Yes, I'm sure.'

Caroline opened the door and they went into her bedroom. It was a large room with white and gilt furniture and a yellow Moroccan cover on the wide bed. Caroline went to the window and closed the yellow curtains. 'This room isn't over-looked,' she said, 'but if I have the curtains drawn it makes me feel more secure.'

She crossed the room and faced him. She was trembling. Simon undid her heavy Moroccan belt and let it drop to the floor. Then he put his hands inside her robe and held her small firm breasts. Caroline did not move, but he could feel that she was quivering. She did not resist when he took the robe off her and she stood before him naked. Her body was perfectly formed. She was one of the most attractive and fascinating girls he had ever seen. He lifted her into his arms and carried her to the bed and laid her down on it. Then he took off his clothes. An instant later he was lying on the bed beside her, stroking her warm, smooth skin.

'I'm frightened,' she whispered to him. 'But I think I'm happier than I've ever been.' Slowly her hand began to explore his body in the faint light that came from the closed curtains.

Then every power of reasoning and all caution left Simon. He only knew that he must try and hurt her as little as possible.

When it happened she gave a little cry of pain. Then her arms went round him and she pressed him deep into her body.

He turned on the bedside lamp and looked at his watch.

'What is it?' Caroline asked, smiling at him.

Simon leaned over and kissed her forehead. 'Oh my darling Caroline,' he said. 'I do so love you, and I don't want to leave you for a moment. But I should get dressed and go down to dinner.'

'Do you want to?' she murmured.

'All I want in the world is to stay with you.' As Simon spoke he realized that his words were true.

Caroline laughed. It was the first time he had ever heard her laugh. 'Very well then,' she said, stretching out her hand to the intercom. She lifted the receiver and dialled a number. 'Is that you, mother?' she asked.

'You know it is,' Betty's voice sounded hoarse and a little

slurred. 'And where is Dr Orville?'

'Here in my apartment,' Caroline said.

'Then tell him to come over here to the living-room. I want to see him.'

'He'll come down later,' Caroline told her.

'Why can't he come now?'

'Because Paul is dining with me tonight. I'm making him supper.'

'"Paul"!' Betty said. 'So you're on Christian name terms with him are you?'

'Yes,' Caroline answered. 'Is there any reason why we shouldn't be?'

'Well, tell your friend Paul that I want to see him.'

'I've told you that I'm making him supper.'

'Is he in the room with you now?'

'No,' Caroline answered. 'I'm speaking from my bedroom.'

Simon was amazed by the calm confidence that Caroline displayed.

'Well, go into the living room,' Betty's voice said, 'and tell him I want to speak to him.'

Simon nodded his head to Caroline and pointed to the living room, for he wanted to talk to Betty in order to avoid an open row between mother and daughter. But Caroline shook her head.

'Can you hear me?' Betty's shrill voice was clearly audible.

'Yes, I can hear you.'

'Then tell Dr Orville I want to speak to him.'

'But he may not want to speak to you.'

'What's that?' Betty demanded. 'How dare you say such things to me? Anyway, what's he been doing all this time?'

To Simon's surprise Caroline gave him a wink. 'That must remain a secret between doctor and patient,' Caroline answered.

'No, it mustn't,' Betty cried. 'It is I who am paying Dr Orville. And it is I who now want to speak to him.'

'He'll be with you at 9 o'clock,' Caroline said.

'But I want him *now*,' Betty insisted.

'I dare say you do,' Caroline answered.

69

'I know you are in one of your moods,' Betty said. 'You're in the kind of mood where you will say or do anything.'

'As it so happens I'm in a very good mood,' Caroline answered. 'But I still don't think it is reasonable that you should have every man in this house,' Caroline concluded and put down the receiver.

She lay back on the bed again and smiled at Simon. 'Now we can make love again,' she said. Then she laughed. 'But don't worry,' she added as she began to stroke his chest. 'Don't worry, I'll still have time to cook you a good supper. But you'll come back after your meeting with my mother. Promise?'

'I'll come back if I can,' Simon answered. 'But don't forget I've got to be beneath your balcony so that I can catch the little Moroccan girl after she has tried to frighten you.'

Caroline stared at him with her large eyes. 'You mean you weren't lying?' she asked. 'You mean that you really did see the girl yourself?'

Simon held her hand against his chest. 'I promise you,' he answered. 'I must get hold of her somehow. She has a key to that little door at the back of the garden – I'm sure of it. Since the doctors are due here very soon I'm almost certain she will appear tonight. And I want to catch her for two reasons. First, I want to prove to you that you don't suffer from any hallucination. Secondly, I want to find out how the girl got the key to the back door and who it is that has planned her apparition. But now let's forget all that and make love again.'

Caroline kissed him, then lay back on the bed. 'Let's,' she said. 'And don't allow my mother to turn you against me.'

'She won't,' Simon assured her. 'Nobody will.'

Yet even as he spoke he felt guilty. He longed to be able to tell her the whole truth so that she knew the fraud he was committing in pretending to be Dr Orville. Each hour his guilt was increased, and now that he had slept with her he longed to share his secret with her. But there was an obvious danger. The knowledge that he had deceived her might destroy her confidence in him and the shock might upset the feeling of security she now appeared to have gained.

Simon was silent. Caroline began stroking his body. 'Now,' she whispered. 'Let's start now.'

Chapter 10

Simon went to his bedroom. Quickly he washed his hands and brushed his hair. Then he walked along the corridor and down the stairs that led to the living room. He opened the door. Betty was standing by the drink cabinet with a glass in her hand. She glanced at her wrist watch.

'I'm glad you're punctual,' she said to him. He could see that she was very angry but trying to control herself. 'It's Sheila's night out, and Toni has driven her into Casablanca so I had to dine alone. But I hope you enjoyed your supper.'

'Yes, I did,' Simon replied.

'I arranged for my darling Caroline to have lessons in cooking when she was only a child. It's an important accomplishment when you're in a country where good servants are difficult to get. How did you find Caroline?'

'I think the tablets are working,' Simon answered. 'By the time the doctors come I have no doubt that Caroline will be declared healthy in mind and body.'

Betty looked at him in silence. 'You were in her apartment for quite a while this evening,' Betty said after a pause. 'What did you talk about?'

'Caroline told me about her childhood,' Simon answered, staring steadily into Betty's protuberant eyes.

'Can that have taken 3 hours?' Betty asked.

'Yes,' Simon said, and took out the snap of Joshua. 'Especially when such items as this are found.'

He saw Betty catch her breath, then she glanced up at him, trying to gauge his expression.

'My dear Dr Orville,' she said, with a gesture of dismissal. 'I admit that I lied to you about that servant. But I did so because all the doctors advised me to. Caroline had become obsessed by him at an early age, so they told me not only to sack him, but to destroy all evidence that he had ever been in my employment. I had no idea that she had kept that photo and obviously treasured it all these years.'

'But if you lied to me about the servant's existence, what other areas have you been untruthful about?' Simon crossed to the drinks cabinet and poured himself out a malt whisky. He had seen her momentary expression of confusion, but now as he turned to face her she was self-assured again.

'Dr Orville, I brought you here to calm Caroline for the ordeal she has to face on her birthday. I did not bring you here to pry into family affairs.'

'But if they have contributed to Caroline's disturbed state of mind, I must know them. Why have other psychiatrists been allowed to know the truth while it is being withheld from me?'

Because you're not a psychiatrist, a voice within him said, and he felt again that skeletal hand of Dr Orville pulling him into the grave. He closed his eyes and drank from his glass.

'I have tried to assist you in every possible way,' Betty said. 'I can see what has happened, Caroline has turned you against me,' Betty crossed her legs and looked defiant, the bulge of her thigh was obscenely white as it showed through the slit in her scarlet caftan.

Simon shook his head. 'No, I am an observer. That is partly my job – to observe the condition of my patient, to enquire into the facts which may have brought that condition about.'

Really, he quite congratulated himself on this professional tone he adopted. Why did it come so easily? Could it be that there was some truth in this destiny wrought by Allah in Ramadan and that the real Dr Orville lived on within him? Again he saw the skeleton and the rotting flesh, and his stomach turned.

He crossed the room and sat down next to her. 'Joshua is a key factor, surely?' Simon asked.

'That is exactly why the doctors told me not to mention his name ever again and always to deny his existence,' Betty looked proudly ahead.

Simon considered this might be a feasible explanation, but he wasn't sure. His lack of professional knowledge foundered on this point. 'The scene Caroline says she observed between you and Joshua. . . .' Simon began. Betty turned and gave him a contemptuous glare. 'Please don't continue. There's not the remotest shred of truth in it. And you insult me by even referring to it.' She looked away again.

'Very well.' Simon had told Caroline that he had proved that her main hallucination was real, yet there was no proof that the traumatic scene with Joshua was true at all. It could have been one of Caroline's sexual fantasies. Yet surely there was nothing so abnormal about that. It was common in adolescents to have fantasies, it might even be a good thing. Certainly it didn't make Caroline unstable now. But as he surveyed Betty he felt sure she was lying.

'Can we talk about Clifton, then? You said yesterday that Clifton had come down to the house in Connecticut and possibly stayed for a night?'

'He came for money to buy his drugs. True.'

'I heard a different story from Caroline. That summer Clifton stayed for many weeks while your husband was in New York.'

Betty sighed. 'Yes, I've heard her story from other doctors. I know how he rode up the stairs naked on a white horse, what an image, don't you think, Dr Orville? An image of male potency, that one. And Clifton of all people,' she laughed. 'What sex he ever had I imagine has been wiped away by his drug addiction.'

Simon sat back on the sofa. 'Caroline said she saw Clifton riding naked on a horse up the main staircase?'

'Oh, was that a detail she missed? Poor girl, you see, Dr Orville, her fantasies take different shapes. I wonder why I'm explaining this to you, for surely in your professional capacity you must have met many cases like this one.' She paused, turning to him smiling with self-righteousness.

'Of course I have, but every case is different.' Simon said the words hurriedly and finished his whisky.

'Then you can tell me more about the nature of the fantasies?' Betty looked sly.

74

Simon's mind went blank. He got up and poured himself out another whisky. He tried to remember what they had been discussing. A white horse. A naked man with long hair. Did Betty know he was an imposter? What was the point of saying anything? Should he escape now? But how could he possibly leave Caroline?

'So I'm being psychoanalysed, am I?' Betty continued. 'The shrink has turned on me.'

He heard Betty's voice, and the tension slowly eased away.

'You think if you're remote and silent I may be forced to reveal things to you? Well, Dr Orville, you're a very attractive man and I've been upset tonight by Caroline's attitude and by your manner.'

He turned with a full glass of whisky. 'I apologize,' he said, inclining his head and switching on his youthful charm. He would be tactful. He must think of something else to say which might not disturb her.

'We also discussed her life in this villa,' Simon said. 'I think it's a lonely life she leads. She ought to get out more often and meet people her own age.'

'And let every young Moroccan boy try to get to bed with her?' Betty asked. She was watching him closely.

'Plenty of Americans and English and French have villas in Casablanca,' Simon replied. 'And anyhow I'm not suggesting she should go out alone. You could send Toni with her.'

'I could,' Betty replied. 'I'll have to think it over. Another point is that Caroline doesn't like going out. She's happier on her own in that apartment.' Betty's eyes were fixed on him. 'Especially when she has a handsome young doctor to spend the evening with her. You've obviously had a success with Caroline. Other doctors who have examined her state of mind have left in despair.'

'Perhaps that's because other doctors have examined her as if she were unbalanced. I have treated her as being stable from the moment we first met, and she has responded to that treatment.'

'How far does your treatment go?' Betty asked. She was still watching him intently.

'It goes far enough for me to be certain that Caroline will be able to face the doctors with confidence,' Simon replied.

'But how long are the effects of your treatment going to last?' Betty enquired. 'I'm sure you're right. I'm certain Caroline will be declared competent. But what happens then? From the way she talked on the telephone it's obvious to me that she has formed an attachment to you. So, say that Caroline is declared healthy. The doctors leave. You are given the other half of your fee. And presumably you will go back to Geneva. But what am I supposed to do if a week later Caroline starts her hallucinations again? That's why I'm asking you how long your treatment will last.'

Simon hesitated.

It seemed that Betty did still believe he was the real Dr Orville. Or was she playing some elaborate game with him? The ground beneath his feet moved now continually as in the earthquake. The real world broke into fragments; he could not tell what was real or unreal, what was true or fake. He must try to cling onto simple statements. Caroline was an anchor.

'I'm certain that if Caroline is treated as a perfectly sane and normal person my treatment will last indefinitely,' he said.

'Even if Caroline doesn't have a handsome doctor looking after her?' Betty asked.

'Yes,' Simon replied. He could see that Betty was still very angry and wanted to accuse him of having seduced Caroline, but she dare not put it into plain words in case he packed up and left. Therefore she did need him, whether he was real or not. Simon had no doubt that Betty would throw him out as soon as the doctors had gone. Caroline would then be 21 and a free agent. The idea now came to him that he could leave the villa taking Caroline with him — if that was what she wanted. He felt intensely protective about her. Perhaps this was yet another sign that he was in love. Or was he doing all he could to make her happy in order to assuage his sense of guilt and to try and drown that terrible image of the dead doctor?

'I'm not at all pleased with the way Caroline talked to me on the telephone this evening,' Betty announced. 'You were in the room next door, but I expect you heard it all?'

'No,' Simon replied. 'But when she came back into the living-room I could see that Caroline was upset.'

'Let's get this straight,' Betty said. 'I don't want your treatment to break the relationship I've had with my daughter.'

What relationship, he thought, it's been nothing but conflict and bitterness.

'Let's get *this* straight,' Simon replied. 'I've no intention of meddling in any way with the relationship between the two of you. You've almost told me in so many words what you suspect me of having done. But I beg you, if I may, to remember that the next few days are crucial to Caroline and to yourself. So, however irritated you may be with Caroline, please do not have a row. I don't want your daughter mentally disturbed, which might arrest her recovery. Incidentally, do you know these two doctors who are flying in from New York?'

'No,' Betty answered. 'I only know their names. One is called Prescot and the other is called Clark, and they're both experts in their field.'

Simon saw a fresh source of danger. 'Would I know them?' he asked.

'I doubt it,' Betty replied.

'Have you informed them that you've got a psychiatrist staying in the house?'

'No,' Betty answered. 'I shall introduce you as Paul Orville, a friend of mine who is staying with me. Besides, little harm is done even if they do find out your profession. I can always tell them that you came here to make a preliminary examination. Anyhow, there is no reason for you to meet them for more than a few minutes.'

'When the doctors are here, give me a hint of what rôle I'm to play, and I'll take it.'

Betty finished the drink in her glass. 'I'm sorry I was cross just now. But I've had rather a trying day and I feel exhausted,' she told him. 'So if you'll excuse me I shall go up to my room and try to get some sleep. Don't worry about the lights. Azziz will switch them off. Help yourself to a drink if you feel like one. But if you'll excuse me I really must retire to bed. Good night to you.'

77

As soon as Betty had left him alone, Simon poured himself another whisky and drank it quickly. Then he left the room but he did not go to his bedroom. He walked to a small door at the end of the patio that led out into the garden; he unlocked it and went out. The lights in his room were switched off, and as he watched Caroline's balcony he saw the lights being turned off in her apartment. He hid himself in a thick clump of mimosa which stood against the wall of the house. There was a long wait. A night bird was calling softly. Presently, in the clear moonlight, he saw a slim figure in white gliding along the wall which led from the small green door at the end of the garden. He did not move. As the figure grew nearer he could see it was the young Moroccan girl without a veil. She approached the bougainvillea which grew up on the trellis-work under Caroline's balcony. Quickly the girl climbed onto the balcony. Faintly he could hear the tapping noise. Then Caroline's lights were switched on. A moment later the girl began her descent from the balcony. Simon waited. As the girl moved through the bushes towards the green door Simon leaped from his shelter and ran to intercept her. The girl saw him and began to run. Simon followed her, but he did not know the pathways. A branch lashed against his face. He stumbled, but he could see the girl was just in front of him. He caught up with her and clutched hold of her arm. In his bad French he tried to speak to her gently, but she stared at him without understanding. She made another frantic struggle to escape. Her robe was torn. He put his arms around her. He could feel the smooth skin of her back. There were no scars on it. And in the moonlight he could see the stripes were smeared. He looked down at his hand and then sniffed it. The smell was of grease paint. Then he heard the sound of a twig snapping just behind him. As he turned he felt a heavy blow on his head, and he lost consciousness.

Chapter 11

As Simon regained consciousness he was first aware of the throbbing at the back of his head and then of the smell of incense which came from a brazier in the middle of the room. He opened his eyes. He was lying on a sofa in a room whose floor and walls were covered with Moorish carpets. Beside each chair was a brass tray on a stand of spindly legs ornately carved. Sitting on a divan and leaning against its cushions was a Moroccan of about 30 who was watching Simon. The man had a thin, clean-shaven face. He was wearing a *djellaba* with gold embroidery. Under his *djellaba* he wore European clothes and very expensive looking snakeskin shoes. When he saw that Simon was staring at him he parted his lips in a wide smile which revealed several gold fillings.

'Do not worry,' he said, speaking English with a strong accent. 'There is nothing to worry about. You are all right. You will have a headache from the blow on your head. But apart from your head and the prick of a needle which was necessary to keep you quiet there is nothing wrong with you.'

'Where am I?' Simon asked.

'You are in my house in Casablanca,' the man answered. 'My name is Mustapha, and I hope that we will be friends,' Once again his lips slid into a smile.

'Why have I been brought here?' Simon asked.

'Let me ask you a question,' Mustapha said. 'Why did you try to get hold of the little Moroccan girl?'

'She was a fake apparition which disturbed my patient. Even the stripes on her body were fake,' Simon answered. 'I wanted to get hold of the girl to prove that she was not a hallucination.'

'By "your patient" you mean Caroline Morrison?'

79

'I do.'

Mustapha nodded his head. 'And you are trying to cure her in time for her examination by doctors on her 21st birthday, which is on March the 9th – very soon now.'

'You seem to know a lot about it.'

Mustapha smiled. 'I do indeed,' he replied. For various reasons it is my intention that the girl should be declared insane, and I may tell you that the girl is definitely insane – without any doubt. I only want to make certain that no mistake should be made.'

'In fact, you are being paid to make sure the girl does go mad,' Simon said.

The door opened and a young man of about Mustapha's age entered the room. Although there was only a slight resemblance, Simon felt instinctively that he was Clifton, Caroline's half-brother. His eyes were a dark blue, and his mouth was less wide. Yet the faint resemblance was undeniable. Perhaps it lay in the nervous expression on his face. His hair was blond and fell onto his shoulders. He looked untidy and dissipated. He was wearing a dirty white T-shirt and stained jeans. His feet were bare. In his right hand he carried a string of amber worry-beads which he clicked together nervously.

Mustapha smiled at him, then turned to Simon. 'Dr Orville,' he said, 'I would like to introduce you to Clifton Morrison, the half-brother of your patient.'

Clifton nodded and stared at Simon. 'You seem to have been quite active since your release from hospital,' he said. 'Unfortunately your energies have been misplaced. Caroline is insane, and all the drugs in the world aren't going to alter that fact.'

'Apart from wishful-thinking, what makes you so sure?' Simon asked.

'We have evidence,' Mustapha said.

'What evidence?' Simon enquired.

'At this stage, we don't intend to disclose our source of information, but you can be assured that the evidence is very reliable.'

Immediately Simon decided that their source might be Sheila

– unless Toni had been heavily bribed.

Clifton stopped playing with his worry-beads. 'You must appreciate that we are aware of your reasons for staying with my step-mother,' he said. 'You must also appreciate that if Betty had no reason to doubt Caroline's sanity it is unlikely that she would pay a large sum of money to send for a specialist from Geneva. You talked just now of "wishful-thinking". Of course it is very much to my advantage that Caroline be declared insane, and therefore legally incompetent, because then I will inherit the Morrison fortune.'

'And, my dear Dr Orville,' Mustapha said, 'it could be very much to your advantage that Caroline Morrison should be found unstable.'

'Why?' Simon asked.

'We know exactly how much money my step-mother is paying you,' Clifton told Simon. 'And now I'm prepared to increase it. I can pay you in cash in almost any currency you choose – if Caroline is proved insane.'

'I don't take bribes,' he said.

'What about the money Betty was paying you?' Clifton asked, clicking his worry-beads. 'Wasn't that a bribe?'

'I admit it was a high fee,' Simon said. 'But it was not a bribe.'

'Not even with the fee being doubled if you succeeded?' Clifton asked.

'I've known such eventualities before now,' Simon said.

'Eventualities of dishonesty?' Clifton asked. 'Eventualities of short-term drugs being used to make a patient appear sane?'

'Certainly,' Simon replied, now growing more confident in his role as Dr Orville. 'But I can assure you that my treatment is not a short-term one. You seem to fail to appreciate that I am an honest man.'

'Are you so sure?' Mustapha asked.

'I don't understand,' Simon said.

'Are you so sure that you are an honest man, Dr Orville?' Mustapha enquired.

'Yes,' Simon replied. 'I am perfectly sure.'

'When we heard you were being contacted by Mrs Morrison

we made some enquiries,' Mustapha said. His sly and cheerful grin seemed almost permanent. 'I visited Geneva myself. Of course, you don't practise now, do you, Dr Orville?'

'Not often,' Simon murmured.

'Not often,' Mustapha echoed. 'Why not, Dr Orville?'

'I came into an inheritance.'

'Precisely. One of your patients. She was also a very wealthy heiress. It would seem that they have an attraction for you, Dr Orville.'

'I don't know what you're implying.' At least he spoke the truth now, Simon thought. His head ached and the smoke from the brazier made his eyes sting. He could not think while they sat there on the embroidered cushions, staring at him with their devious smiles.

'He doesn't know what we're implying,' Clifton said with a laugh. 'Come off it, doctor. There was quite a scandal, wasn't there? She committed suicide, she took an overdose. At the inquest it was suggested that as you were the sole benefactor of her Will you may even have implanted the idea.'

'The case was very complicated,' Simon said, saying the first thing that entered his mind.

'Not when your secretary gave her evidence. She had overheard the last session with your patient, who was in love with you, and also hysterical. Your secretary said that you were quarrelling. Hardly the professional bedside manner was it now, Dr Orville?'

'My secretary was jealous. Her evidence was unreliable.'

Simon didn't know what he was saying; he was creating a fictional court case. But what did it matter? They must have only heard rumours; there could be nothing substantial, no real facts.

'You drove your patient Miss White home to her lakeside villa. Your car was seen parked in her driveway until one in the morning. She was found dead by her maid when she brought in her mistress's breakfast. Time of death on the Coroner's report was around 3 a.m.' Mustapha leaned back on the cushion resting his chin in his hand. He surveyed Simon quietly.

'Where is all this leading?'

'It means you're a crook, Dr Orville,' Clifton said. 'You've done it once, and every criminal when he gets away with one crime has an obsessional desire to do it again. When you heard from my step-mother it must have seemed like fate playing right into your hands.'

'I don't understand,' Simon cried out.

'Dear, dear,' Clifton murmured, glancing at Mustapha. 'He doesn't understand. Have you forgotten your evening of romantic love? Can you be such a cynic, Dr Orville? Can you deny that you were in my step-sister's bedroom for some hours? She pulled the curtains, didn't she?'

'Who is it who is spying on us there?' Simon asked in a rage.

'We're not likely to tell you,' Mustapha said. 'But such evidence surely indicates that your romantic attachment to your new patient means that you have a plan to inherit the Morrison fortune.'

'That's nonsense . . . .'

'Is it?' Clifton asked, he got up and stood over Simon. 'She's a young and innocent kid, she's also as mad as a hatter. You must know that with all your professional experience of rich loonies, doctor? She could marry you and then after a few months you'd push her over the edge. It's happened before and you got away with it.'

Simon looked down at his hands, they were shaking. So was the real Dr Orville a criminal? Had he taken on an identity which was not the respectable one he had thought? It was ironic and he might have laughed if he had not felt so trapped.

'I demand to be released from here,' he said sullenly. 'You have no right to kidnap me and then threaten me.'

Mustapha slowly fanned the air with his broad hand and said: 'There is a vast fortune involved. Now, let us talk business. You will make sure, Dr Orville, without any doubt at all, that Caroline will appear insane when she sees the specialists from New York. For that service we will treble your fee. Surely a handsome offer?'

'And how am I to ensure that Caroline appears insane?'

Clifton laughed. 'My dear doctor, we know you have ways. It

shouldn't prove difficult for you at all.'

'And if I refuse?' His mind was still dead but he must play along with them for the time.

'We shall reopen, as it were, the old court case, for we have in our possession new evidence which will ensure a conviction.' It was Mustapha who had spoken and his dark ebony eyes stared at Simon with a fanatic's gleam.

'What new evidence?'

'A written confession from Miss White's maid,' Clifton said.

'Saying?'

'That you paid her a sum of money to say that you left the house at eight in the evening. It was her evidence that saved you. It's strange,' Mustapha said, rising, 'that you did not correct our earlier statement that the car was seen parked in the drive way until I a.m. for no one else knew that except you and the maid.'

'I've got a filthy headache,' Simon said angrily. 'How the hell do you think I can work anything out after being knocked over the head?'

'Then we shall have a long night ahead of us, Mustapha answered.

There was a pause. A boy shuffled in carrying Turkish coffee and laid the tray at Mustapha's feet. He poured out the dark thick liquid into three cups. Simon sipped his: it was so hot it burned his tongue, but the sweetness seemed to clear his head a little. Clifton handed him a glass of water and a saucer of three green sticky fruits. He sipped the water and declined the fruit. A fly crawled over it.

Mustapha got up, then paused at the door. 'I have business to attend to. Keep Dr Orville company, Clifton, I'm sure it won't take long for you to persuade him.'

Simon heard the menace in the voice and glancing at Clifton saw that the young man had swallowed nervously, as if he too was now afraid. Clifton picked up a long stemmed pipe and lit the bowl; gradually the smell of kif filled the room, mixed with incense. The air now seemed thick with spices.

'I only want justice for myself,' Clifton said, staring at Simon.

'Your father's Will was explicit. If that was his wish you can't change it.'

'Too many damned misunderstandings in those last years, If I could have seen my father it would have been all right.' He paused. 'Look, you haven't any choice. That tap on the head Mustapha gave you was nothing. If you don't agree . . . well, he's not patient, you know. I can more or less see your future and it isn't a long one. Don't blame me. It's not my choice. . . .'

'What are you saying?' Simon broke in.

'The next blow on the head will be fatal, that's what I'm saying. You'll be taken back to that villa and you'll be a corpse. They'll find you in the morning in the patio, it will seem as if you've fallen from your balcony. As simple as that. So face up to the facts, for that's what they are.' He closed his eyes and inhaled the smoke.

Simon got up, for one moment he thought of escape; of walking out of the room, out of the house, out of Casablanca, Morocco itself, perhaps even out of Orville's identity. But he stood still and looked around the room. It was too difficult. There would be servants in the compound. Besides, he was guilty either as Dr Orville or as Simon Perry.

Clifton opened his eyes. 'Well?'

'I agree,' Simon said. 'What else can I do? But exactly what do I do? Would you tell me that?'

Mustapha returned, perhaps he had been listening? He looked pleased and rubbed his hands. 'You stop interfering, Dr Orville,' Mustapha said, 'and if you see anything odd or strange happening, ignore it. We will contact you, if and when we need you.' Mustapha gave him a mock bow. 'One of my servants will drive you back to the villa. And don't waste your time talking to him, he is a deaf mute. Good night, Dr Orville.'

Simon glanced down at Clifton. He appeared to be dozing.

'Good night,' Clifton said.

Chapter 12

Simon longed for sleep, he longed for his unconscious to overwhelm him, to wipe out everything he had experienced in the last week. Yet as he lay in his bed in Betty's villa he was also frightened of that same unconscious, frightened of the dead, mocking figure of Dr Orville who might return to him in sleep. There was so much to disentangle. So many unanswerable questions. He must consider them. He must. It was 4 o'clock in the morning. He must warn Caroline. He had to save her. Yes, of course. Somehow in all this labyrinth he would do the honest thing, he might at last save his own integrity.

Azziz woke him from a deep sleep at eight. He laid a tray of coffee and croissants upon a table by Simon's bed. He was about to leave the room when Simon spoke to him. He felt refreshed and suddenly clear-headed. 'Bring me more coffee Azziz. And tell Miss Morrison that I shall join her within the hour.'

Azziz bowed.

Simon cleaned his teeth, sipped the hot coffee, then showered and shaved. He drank more coffee, dressed and then paced the room. So Mustapha had gone to Geneva. If he had gone to Geneva would it not have been likely that he might have seen the real Dr Orville and so know that Simon was an imposter? The story of the inquest. Was that true, or had they made it up? If there was such a scandal was it likely that Betty would contact him and bring him over here? Mustapha might not have seen him in Geneva. Betty might not have heard of the scandal. Nothing held together in this world which had been shattered by an earthquake.

But then in the end Mustapha and Clifton were not relying on blackmailing him over the past inquest but on a threat of murder. He cursed himself for not asking Clifton about Betty, for not checking up on that story. Even if Clifton had not told him the truth about Betty, he would have seen his reactions; there might have been some clue to the truth in his behaviour.

Who was spying on him in the villa? Who had seen Caroline's curtains being closed last evening? Both Sheila and Toni had gone out. That left Betty and the servants. Unless . . . he could ask what time they had gone out.

Why shouldn't he take Caroline out in the spare car today? They would drive away. Once away from the villa he might see things in perspective. Someone must be intending to drug Caroline on the day the specialists arrive. Her own stories of those days when she became disorientated implied that she was taking some hallucinogenic drug without knowing it. He must tell her not to eat or drink anything which she hadn't prepared herself. The orange juice was mixed by Sheila. What else? She drank vodka occasionally, sometimes Campari, that was bitter enough to disguise any additive. But who stood to gain most from disinheriting her? Clifton obviously, if Betty's account of the legacy was true. But then why should she take so much trouble to prove to the specialists that Caroline was sane? *But she was sane.* Surely she was sane? Clifton didn't think so. Clifton believed in the legacy.

He ran out of the room and down the steps into the patio. He knocked loudly at Caroline's door, she called to him to enter. She was in a green silk dress and she was tying her hair back with a ribbon of the same colour.

'I thought . . .' she began to say, then saw that Simon had his finger to his lips.

'I thought the same,' Simon said. 'Let's take a walk by the pool.' He opened the door, she frowned a little, then as she passed him she gave his cheek a kiss.

A servant was sweeping the dead petals into the flowerbeds. Simon took her arm and they walked the other side of the pool towards two bamboo chairs. 'Your room is possibly bugged,' he said, 'I don't want to take any chances.'

'You look awful,' she murmured. 'As if you've had the most

ghastly nightmare.'

'I have.'

'The girl was there last night. I heard a scuffle and I rushed out into the garden. I thought I would have seen you.'

'You just missed me by seconds I should think. My unconscious body was being hauled off by a Moroccan.'

Caroline stared at him for a moment, then clutched his arm. 'Oh Paul, how terrible. Are you hurt? What happened? We must call the police. Why haven't you?'

He shook his head and smiled. 'You know that didn't occur to me. But now you've said it, I can't see it will do much good. My word against theirs. And knowing the Moroccan police I can see that someone will bribe them and we'd get nowhere. Now, I want us to drive out of this place and get away today. It will be good for you. Maybe we can take a picnic. No, that's no good. I've sworn to myself that you mustn't eat anything which you haven't prepared yourself.'

'Then I'll make the picnic. But tell me first what happened?'

'I'll tell you later.' He got up from the chair, then bent down and kissed the top of her head. 'You've become very precious to me, do you know that?' She got up and flung her arms around him. He disentangled her. 'Someone is bound to be watching in this place. Look, you throw some goodies together and I'll get a car. I'll have to see your mother first and tell her what we're doing.'

He hurried back into the house. He found Betty in the living room giving orders to Toni. He lingered by the open door for a moment and listened.

Betty's voice was harsh. 'So you think the police won't watch that house? Haven't I given them *enough* money? Don't I get the protection I've paid for, Toni?'

He heard Toni's answer, his voice was patient. 'I keep telling you, Betty, Mustapha has grown rich on every illicit trade going in our country. He has the police in the palm of his hand. If Clifton has him behind him, then they'll stop at nothing to get the inheritance.'

'Oh my God,' Betty cried out as Simon entered. She turned.

'Good morning, Dr Orville, we were discussing my criminal step-son.'

'I don't want to disturb you,' Simon said. 'But I just came in to mention I'm taking Caroline out for a drive today.'

Betty stared at him for a moment in silence. Then she sat down. 'That's all I needed.' Then she glanced up at Toni. 'I'm sorry, but it's out of the question. Caroline must stay here.'

'As my patient, I strongly suggest that such a trip would be beneficial for her.'

'Caroline never wants to go anywhere,' Betty said sharply.

'She does now. I shall continue the treatment throughout the day. I think it best she gets away from this villa.'

'She's protected here. There are servants. No-one can get into this villa without Toni knowing.'

Simon suppressed a smile.

'She could be kidnapped,' Betty cried out, almost tearfully.

'If they, whoever they are, had decided to kidnap Caroline, they would have done it before now.'

There was silence for a moment. Betty stared at him and frowned. Then Toni spoke. 'I think it would be best if Miss Morrison stayed here, Dr Orville.'

'I don't,' Simon said decisively. 'How am I to do what you asked me, to treat Caroline, when you hinder me in this manner?' He turned. 'This is highly unprofessional and I have never worked before under these conditions. Nor, Mrs Morrison, will I endure them. I shall make plans to fly back to Geneva this afternoon.' He began to walk from the room. At least, he thought, such a decision might throw some light on how they thought of him. He had got to the door when Betty's voice detained him.

'No, Dr Orville, please. . . .'

He turned. 'I shall of course return your fee.' That was a grand touch; he rather cared for that.

'If Toni came with you. There must be some protection. Can't you see my nerves? I'm suffering from such fears. Please Dr Orville, can't you sympathize with me?' Betty dabbed her eyes with a lace-edged handkerchief.

Simon looked at Toni and sighed. 'As long as it is understood that my conversations with my patient are in confidence between us.'

Toni agreed. The three of them got into the car with the picnic hamper Caroline had made. Toni drove further inland, across dusty plains towards rolling hills, a cluster of gleaming white walls and lopsided roofs pierced by minarets and domes which seemed to cling precariously to an outcrop of jagged rock which heralded the uplands. Toni pointed out the town. 'It is another holy city. One of our saints founded it and used it as a base for a Holy War against the Christian colonies along the coast.' Toni chuckled. 'For five centuries every European near would have been caught, then hung up by his ears until he died.'

Simon remembering last night felt that Morocco had not changed much over the centuries. He sat in the back and held Caroline's hand. Peasants were scattered over the thin soil, their backs bent, they did not bother to look up at the car as it passed.

'We will stop there for a while, it is market day. From before dawn the peasants have travelled there bringing their produce. You'll see,' Toni said, slamming his foot down on the accelerator so that a cloud of reddish dust obscured the view.

A fortress with battlements stood beside the grand Mosque in the market square, its high walls pitted with age, scarred with ancient battles, yet the sun shining from a vividly blue sky made the building glow gold, as if its source was spiritual and not a war of vengeance.

When they got out of the car they were surrounded by small boys begging. Toni shouted to them and they scattered. He said protectively to Caroline, 'You're all right with me. Without me, you would be pestered all the time, until you had emptied your pockets.'

Caroline looked around her in amazement. Near them an old man sat on the cobblestones outside the open door of his shop. He was surrounded by earthen jars, each holding many kif pipes, their clay bowls no bigger than thimbles. Simon recognised the same type that Clifton had used in the night. Two small girls stared at them from the shadowy doorway and giggled nervously. The small square was crammed with people. Women sat cross-legged, surrounded by their wares! Mounds of chick peas, lentils, eggs, dried figs, pears, herbs, sprigs of mint and parsley, oregano and thyme. A man was selling milk from tall terracotta jars; a sprig of oleander stoppered the long neck of each full jar; his customers lined up with jugs waiting for him to pour the fresh milk. Another man held a tray of butter, each pat decorated with a five-pointed star. Customers haggled and bargained; the noise of shouting voices was deafening. Caroline tugged Simon's sleeve and pointed out a small boy who deftly stole from each stall, an egg there, a date from a mound, a hard green pear, each object disappeared into his dirty *djellaba* with a conjuror's art. A cripple, calling for alms in a high pitched voice, inched his way through the market. He wore a leather apron tied beneath him and pushed himself forward by his hands which were encased in leather boots.

'Let's go,' Caroline said. 'I never imagined. . . .'

Water melons were being sliced and laid out in rows. Their bright pink flesh decorated with black seeds seemed to echo the tiny black windows which dotted the high walls of the houses. Suddenly Caroline echoed Simon's thought. 'I feel I'm being watched, even here,' she whispered and held Simon tightly for a second. Toni paused and bought a slice of melon, throwing down a coin.

They passed a mule hung down with pots and panniers. Lashed to his back were rolls and cane baskets. The mule shifted his hooves uneasily as if he could stand no more.

'Why did you bring us here?' Caroline asked Toni. 'I can't stand people.'

Toni was silent. Simon steered Caroline gently back to the car. 'I expect Toni wanted to show us the holy city,' he said. 'Now, we'll find somewhere peaceful.'

They drove further up into the hills. Toni turned off the road and on to a mud track. After a few moments he parked the car. He nodded. 'It's all right, we have not been followed.' He pointed. 'You're quite safe, have your picnic, there's a small mountain path which leads to a sacred spring. There's no other way of getting to it. And I can see anyone who would climb up the same way.'

Once they were out of sight of Toni and the car, it was different. They both felt the freedom and she turned to him, clinging to him. They kissed, then turned to look at the view. Beyond in the far distance they could still see the ocean, but the horizon merged into the blue sky and the land below them showed areas of red earth, then tawny rock flecked with green, patches of yellow maize and clumps of silver green olives.

The spring bubbled out of the rock; around it tall grass grew, amongst the grass wild anemones flowered and tiny irises no taller than a thumb. They both drank from the spring, splashing water onto their faces. Above them tiny white rags fluttered on the branches of an olive tree. They sat in the shade, their backs to the tree.

'Now you can tell me what happened,' Caroline said.

Simon told her, but he simplified the story by omitting all mention of the inquest and the scandal over the heiress. She buried her face in his chest and he held her very tightly. 'What a terrible thing. Thank God, you're safe. But poor Clifton . . . what has happened to him that he should be like that?'

He spoke to her gently. 'Look Caroline, we haven't much time. I intend that the specialists will consider you legally competent. My God, I think you're the only healthy person in that villa.'

'And you,' she said.

'If you want a drink, stick to champagne, they can't poison that.'

She laughed. 'I packed some.' She opened the hamper and brought out a bottle, then bread and a tin of paté. They ate as they talked.

'I must try and eliminate who it could be that is spying on you. Now, we'll start. . . .'

'With a toast,' she said, raising her glass. 'To us, my love. They say that patients fall in love with their psychiatrists. I even read somewhere that it was part of the treatment.' She smiled. 'Go on.'

'Now we'll start with your mother,' he stressed.

'Must you spoil a beautiful moment?'

'Caroline please, we have a little time alone, we must consider all the possibilities. Now, this is how I understand it. Because of your childhood accusations about her to your father, she had to get in doctors to prove that these were fantasies so as to clear herself?' Caroline nodded. 'I imagine she thought your father would leave all his wealth to her and not to you?' Caroline shrugged. 'Anyway we have the Will. When it was read out to you what exactly did it say?'

'I don't know. It never was.'

'But it must have been. That's a legal requirement.'

Caroline sighed. 'When Daddy died, I was in despair. You don't know how deeply I loved him. He was everything to me. I wept for weeks. I didn't care a damn about wills or anything. It was like being in a black abyss.'

'So you can't remember even a lawyer's letter?' She shook her head. 'Then you only know about the Will from what Betty has told you?'

'Yes.'

'Okay, let's suppose that if they say you're insane, not competent, the inheritance may then be shared between Clifton and your mother. Which brings me to this point. If that's true, then why should Betty bring me over from Geneva? She has to clear herself for someone, to show someone that she has done all she can for you. Why does she want me to stay on when the specialists are there?'

'One of them, Dr Prescot, was a friend of Daddy's.' Caroline looked at Simon. 'Is that a clue?'

'Betty told me she didn't know the specialists,' Simon answered. 'I suppose it's possible that your father had friends whom neither you nor your mother had ever met. But she also told me that she wouldn't necessarily introduce me as a psychiatrist who had examined you.' He paused. 'But if they conclude you are not competent because of the hallucinations, then I think that's exactly what she would do – because she would want every bit of proof she could lay hands on that she did everything in her

93

power to have you cured.'

'So mother is a prime suspect?'

'Everyone is a damned suspect, it seems to me. If it's Betty then Toni would be in her pay. Now, we'll put Betty in the clear. I overheard a conversation this morning, and I hardly think they put that on for my benefit. But it showed that Betty is terrified of what Clifton and Mustapha might do. As we don't know the details of the Will, it could all be bound up with that.'

'You sound more like a detective than a psychiatrist,' she said and kissed him on the lips.

'If it's not Betty who is allied with Clifton, then it must be Sheila or a servant. Azziz, for example.'

'I've never liked Sheila. My instinct says it's her,' Caroline said cheerfully.

'You're amazing,' he said laughing. 'For one who might be plunged into insanity by some devious scheme, you seem to take it all so lightly.'

'It's because you're going to protect me,' she murmured, snuggling close to him.

They were content. For an hour they lay there within their own happiness, untouched by all the threats which surrounded them. 'You know,' Simon said at last, 'I think it would be a good thing if we all ate dinner together tonight.'

'Why?' she murmured dreamily, doing up the buttons of his shirt.

'I'd like them to see how calm and happy you are. I'd like us both to watch their reactions.'

'But I'm not supposed to eat anything which I haven't prep. . . .' He placed his hand over her mouth.

'They can hardly poison us all, can they?'

Chapter 13

When Toni had parked the car at the villa, Simon had told him that Caroline would be dining with them that evening. He then took Caroline back to her apartment. She stood framed in the doorway. 'Thank you Paul, thank you.' She kissed him and as he clung to her, he closed the door. No woman had made him feel so relaxed and happy, no woman had made him so completely himself, and yet he was disguised as another man and she sometimes seemed more girl than woman. She drew him into the room with her hands. 'I feel so happy, such a wonderful day, we must do it tomorrow too. But no towns, just somewhere beautiful and quiet.'

He laughed. 'Didn't Toni's story of the djinn worry you?'

'But no, because it was a good djinn. I'm positive.'

'But we didn't hang a rag as an offering that made the djinn good. Or leave a lighted candle.'

'We left a fragment of our love, I think'. She turned away from him to the drinks tray. 'Now, before I shower I feel like a Campari. How about you?'

'Why not? Anything you say.' He watched her lovingly as she poured the red liquid into two glasses, then suddenly he came to his senses. 'No, Caroline – I forgot, you mustn't touch it.' He took the glass from her and smelled it. The bitter aroma was there, but it might possibly have hidden something else.

'Oh really Paul, you're becoming as paranoiac as I used to be.'

'They drug you somehow,' he almost shouted. 'Don't you believe me?'

'Well, I'm not likely to drink Campari for breakfast before the specialists see me.'

'Then it has to be the orange juice.' He kissed her. 'Lock the door, I'll come and fetch you for dinner.' He crossed the patio and went towards the door in the wall; it was well screened by mimosa and honeysuckle. He noticed the lock had been oiled, but above and below he saw there were two rusty bolts. He forced them to close, swearing at the effort and grazing his fingers. Then he lugged two large stones which had fallen from the wall and placed them in front of the door. No-one would get in that way tonight, he thought.

It was only when he returned to his own room that he realized they had been indiscreet in Caroline's apartment. He had been so careful that morning, but the sun, their love and a day out from the villa, had made him careless. Well, he shrugged, perhaps Caroline was right, he *was* paranoiac. Bugging her room was taking things too far. He threw off his clothes and showered, then found himself shaking his head, thinking that if they threatened murder they were capable of anything. If anyone had heard their conversation they would now know he intended to be honest, that he was not a pawn of Clifton's, that he had decided Caroline was sane and would do all he could to prove her so.

Betty's whole manner had changed since that morning. She sat at the head of the table and smiled at her daughter. She exuded relief and pleasure, she constantly thanked Simon for his treatment. 'I can tell that his "wonder drug" has just done wonders for you, my darling. Don't you think so, Sheila?'

'Yes, Mrs Morrison.' Sheila smiled also, but Simon felt it was false, as he always had done.

'What amount do you give her, Dr Orville?' Betty asked.

'Just two a day, mother,' Caroline said. 'One in the morning and one at night.' Caroline smiled, but did not glance at Simon. Instead she had looked at Sheila and noticed her stiffen. Simon exhaled a small sigh of relief, he had quite forgotten the sleeping pills. But what did it matter? Caroline seemed determined to protect him.

Simon addressed Sheila. 'Did you have an enjoyable evening yesterday?'

'Thank you, yes,' she answered, without looking up from her plate.

Azziz refilled their wine glasses, but Caroline shook her head and placed her hand over her glass. 'What do you do in Casablanca, Sheila?' Caroline asked.

'I see a film, generally.'

'What film did you see last night?' Caroline asked.

'A French film. *Les Jeux Interdits . . .*' Sheila said without pausing.

But Caroline had interrupted her. 'Oh yes, I remember, we saw it last year, mother. It's about those children that play with death. They have a cemetery and then there's that music.' She turned to Sheila.

'Didn't you see it with us last year?'

'Oh, I may have done,' Sheila rose. 'I'm sorry, I've got a headache, will you excuse me?'

Betty stared at her, she nodded in an irritable manner. When Sheila had left the room she said: 'Well really, I've never seen her so jumpy. You were only making polite conversation, Caroline. Why should she react like that?'

Toni said: 'Perhaps she has a secret lover in Casablanca and doesn't want us to know.'

'She's far too fat and ugly,' Betty said, tossing her napkin onto the table. 'We'll have coffee in the living room, Azziz.'

It was over coffee and liqueurs that the lights suddenly went out. Betty swore furiously, calling for Azziz. Toni apologised in the dark to Simon and said that sometimes power cuts did occur, but they only lasted for a few minutes. Azziz brought in oil lamps and in the soft light Simon thought he had never seen Caroline looking so beautiful. But she said she was tired and Simon escorted her back to her own apartment. They kissed in the dark. He whispered. 'Lock your room, and if you hear any noises in the night, ignore them.'

'I promise,' she said. 'I feel so safe with you now.'

He returned to the living room. The lights were still out. Betty was restless. 'I think we all ought to go to bed. Toni, this is ridiculous. It's now nearly an hour that we've been plunged into darkness.' Betty got up. 'Good night, Dr Orville. Azziz will have put candles in your room. I'll see you in the morning.'

When Simon entered his room he saw that an ornate candelabra stood on the wooden chest. Its five candles with their orange flames sent gigantic shadows over walls and ceiling, changing the shapes of the furniture, so that for a moment the room seemed peopled with looming giants, who then in the next second vanished.

Simon felt an overwhelming exhaustion. The day had been long and he had drunk too much, and perhaps had had too much sun. He stood in the room for a moment and closed his eyes against these changing shadows. He began to waver on his feet; he knew he must undress at once, for he would then fall into a heavy sleep. With relief he felt the cool marble beneath his naked feet. He hauled on his pyjamas, then began to cross the room to enter his bathroom.

The candles sent another black shadow across the bathroom door; it hovered there for a moment quivering, then the door began to open. Slowly the door swung open by itself. The shadow moved. But still the door opened, edging its way in an arc, as if slowly, inch by inch, the door was being pushed open by someone inside the bathroom who was weak, had little strength and was pitting what strength he had against that door.

Simon had stopped moving. He was watching the door in alarm. When it had first moved, and begun to swing outwards, he had thought Mustapha was hidden there. But now he thought Mustapha was trying to frighten him.

So he stood, unmoving in that vast candle-lit room, watchful and in suspense. But then, at that moment when the door was fully open, he saw a dim, huddled shape. Not Mustapha, or any man, could be this shape.

Someone, or something, was huddled in a wheel chair. It must be a chair, for it moved without sound towards him. Simon stepped back. Then as the candlelight moved across the shape he saw more details.

In the chair sat a man, or the remnants of one. He wore torn and filthy clothes, his body was half-bandaged and the bandages were dirty and blood-stained. His face was so haggard, the eyes which now stared up at Simon bulged from the flesh as if his head had become a skull already. He stretched out his bony hands towards Simon, as the chair moved inexorably towards him. The face seemed distorted by suffering, but still Simon recognized the face: he recognized the face he had seen in his nightmare.

The shape that moved so slowly towards him was the *real* Dr Orville.

Simon heard himself mutter. 'No, no, no.' The sound came from the back of his throat, and he was conscious that he was retreating away from the chair and this phantom huddled in it. He was being haunted by the man whose identity he had stolen.

Simon went on walking backwards, then his body hit the chest and he turned and picked up the candelabra. He held it high above him. The chair stopped about 3 feet away from Simon. In the candle light he could now see more details of this phantom, the face with its scaly grey skin smudged with dark bruised blotches, the scarred scalp coagulated with dried blood, fringed with dirty white hair. The *real* Dr. Orville didn't have white hair, Simon thought. But this was not the real Dr Orville, there was nothing real about this horrifying apparition. But the chair must be real, he thought. Simon took a step forward. He must confront what was haunting him. He must touch the chair. And then he would touch this creature too.

But whatever it was in the chair now thrust itself upwards. Wavering for a second, it still clung to the chair and then it lifted its arms out towards Simon. It spoke in a voice cracked with thirst and anguish. 'Help me, Simon Perry. For pity's sake, help me.'

'You're dead,' Simon whispered. 'Dead, bloody dead.'

The smell of dirt and decay was in the room. Simon stepped back, still holding the candelabra above him, its light still shedding those gigantic shadows over the room. The apparition moved its head, as if denying what Simon had whispered. Its hands stretched out imploringly. Simon stared at the skeletal hands which were trying to clutch him, to cling on to him as in the dream. Then Simon knew what he must do. He must destroy this ghost.

He would hurl the candelabra at the figure. He would burn it away. The flames would kill it in whichever world it existed, even if it was in his own mind.

Simon took another step back, his hand gripped the candelabra, his arm was high and with all his force he threw it at the apparition. But at the same time the wounded ghost collapsed; it seemed to crumple in a dusty heap of rags upon the floor and the candelabra hit the wheel chair, knocking it backwards. Two of the candles flickered and went out. Then the candelabra rolled off the chair, hitting the marble tiled floor. The ghost groaned; it moved again, as if now about to crawl towards Simon, but one of his claw-like hands fell on a flame and snuffed the last candle and in that moment Simon turned.

He ran from the room. He ran down the corridor, down the marble staircase which led to the living room, he ran through the open door where an oil lamp still sent its amber glow over the room. Toni sat there alone, drinking a whisky and soda. He looked up with amazement as Simon entered the room.

'What is it, Dr Orville?' Toni asked.

Simon stood there, trying to get back his breath. Then the electric lights came back on.

Toni laughed. 'You see, the power cuts are never for long. About an hour and a half, that one.' He stood up and came over to Simon. 'Is there something you forgot? Can I help you?'

Simon stared at Toni. Perhaps in this villa hallucinations were infectious?

'I wouldn't mind a nightcap,' Simon murmured. His hands were shaking.

'Help yourself,' Toni said. 'I'm off to bed.'

Toni turned the wick of the oil lamp down, then saying goodnight he left the room. Simon had poured himself a large brandy. His hands were still shaking. He crossed the room and closed the door. He looked about the well-lit space, and listened to the silence; there were only the cicadas still rasping, and soon they would die if they had not mated.

He sat down on the sofa and gulped a mouthful of brandy. It stung his mouth. He rolled the spirit around his palate and then swallowed it.

Was he being sent insane by his own crime, he wondered? He drank the rest of the brandy. It calmed and soothed a little of the shock, but his hands still quivered and he got up and poured himself another drink. His mouth was dry, horribly dry, as it had felt in the earthquake, as that voice of the phantom was dry when it croaked. Dry and lifeless, like the last dead cicada which soon would fall from the eucalyptus tree.

The phrase *the dividing line* came into his mind. He wondered, where did you draw the line between life and death? Where was the line between the mad and the sane? Did that line exist? Could anyone know what was real and what was illusion? Had he dreamed that whole horrible experience? Did it exist because of his own subjective guilt over his crime? Then he, like his patient, had created his own hallucination? But he had proved that Caroline's hallucinations were reality.

He sipped at his brandy, made himself comfortable on the sofa, and tried to arrive at some clear conclusion. But there was nothing. Since that earthquake, his world had been shattered into inexplicable fragments. He was lost among jigsaw pieces, none of which would ever fit together.

In the morning Azziz found Simon still there. He had fallen asleep on the sofa. His sleep had been dreamless, there had been no nightmares. He now felt refreshed and returned to his room. The servants had already cleaned it. The candelabra had disappeared. Simon could not believe that the vision had occurred at all. But when he thought about it, his arm with the torn ligament still shook and he began to fear that he might be sent insane by his crime. In the ruins of Agadir they were still finding people after 10 days who were alive, hauling them wounded, starving and semi-conscious from their imprisonment. Suppose the real Dr Orville was still trapped and that ghost he had seen had been projected by the living Orville? No, he was dead: he had seen Orville crushed. Then the dead man was haunting him. How could he live with that fear? He must leave Morocco, perhaps then the visions would cease. But ghosts continued to haunt their victims wherever they went. There was no escape for him.

He paced his room, trying to control his nerves. You've taken on this man's identity and now he has returned to you. His ghost will not rest until you give him back his name and life, until you say to the world again that you're Simon Perry. *You are not Dr Orville.*

But what about Caroline? They loved each other. He was certain of that. For the first time in his life he had found a woman to love and who returned that love. How could he turn his back on that? If he told Caroline the truth she would despise him, he would lose her. That thought terrified him too.

There was a light tap on his door and he froze. Then it opened and Caroline entered.

'I thought I'd visit you for a change. Besides, you're late,' she said smiling.

They hugged each other.

'Is anything the matter?' she whispered. 'You're trembling.' He nodded. 'I think I am,' he whispered. 'But in your arms it's better.'

Caroline laughed. 'But why?'

'Bad dreams,' he said. He told her that he was still haunted in his sleep by the Agadir earthquake, that he thought it would continue for months, he told her of the terror he felt of being buried alive and that sometimes in his sleep he returned to those dreadful black and silent hours.

She consoled him, whispering loving phrases, stroking his brow, giving his nose, eyelids, cheeks, tender kisses. She seemed like the morning sun filling a dark and airless cell.

'And I've got something funny to tell you,' she said. 'I just passed Sheila, and she's got band aid plasters on both hands. I asked her what had happened and she just glared at me.'

Simon stared down at his own hands. The grazes from pulling the rusty bolts into place still showed on his fingers.

Caroline followed his gaze. 'How did you do that?'

'I think possibly the same way that Sheila did. Come on. Let's look.'

They went out to the patio and towards the garden wall. The bolts on the door had been pulled back and the stones he had placed there had been rolled away. He turned to Caroline. 'Last night, did you hear the tapping again?'

'Yes. But I refused to put my lights on. I did as you told me.'

'And then?'

'Nothing. I must have slept.'

They turned and walked down by the swimming pool, sitting in the shade of a palm tree. There was not a breath of wind. The sun blazed down from a cloudless sky. The world seemed still and perfect.

Caroline spoke. 'You wanted me to dine *en famille* last night, so as to see people's reactions. What did you think?'

Simon's mind was far away. Telling Caroline about the earthquake and his nightmares had almost convinced him that he had dreamed that horrible experience last night. It could have been so, he told himself, yesterday I drank too much, maybe I even took a couple of those sleeping pills. I went to bed, fell at once into a deep sleep and then had the nightmare. I ran from the room and saw Toni in the living room, drank half of a brandy and then fell asleep again. It was almost as if I had been drugged too.

Caroline tugged at his sleeve. 'Answer me.'

He turned to her. 'Yes. Your mother convinced me that she's utterly innocent. She looked so delighted with you.'

Caroline took off her sunglasses, stared at him for a moment and then said with a smile: 'She's either innocent or else she's a brilliant actress. Maybe with all those theatrical friends she has, some of the dramatic art has rubbed off on her.'

'Maybe it has,' he echoed. But Simon was unconvinced. Then he remembered something he had wanted to ask Caroline.

'Did you ever see Clifton riding on a white horse up the stairs of the Connecticut house? Oh yes,' he added, 'Clifton was naked.'

Caroline replaced her sun glasses, she stared at him for a moment through the dark lenses and then burst out laughing. 'Oh Paul, you've got to be kidding. Betty didn't tell you that I said that, did she?'

'Yes, she did.' He frowned down at the clear water in the

103

swimming pool.

'Then my dear mother is lying. Look Paul, I think she wants me to inherit the fortune, because she needs that third of the money. But in the past she certainly had to make me seem to have these hallucinations, or else her so-called love affairs would have made father divorce her. Betty has always loved money. That and sex are her two obsessions.'

Simon nodded. 'Then she lied to me. And what's more, Caroline, she lies so well she *is* a good actress.'

'What did I tell you,' Caroline said triumphantly. 'So how do we assess last night?'

Simon groaned. 'How the hell do I know?'

'Forget it,' she said. 'Let's swim.'

They spent the morning swimming and sun bathing next to the pool. Toni had lent Simon a costume and they relaxed happily together. Both of them erased from their minds all the mystery which threatened them. For they were secure in each other's happiness.

Betty came down to the pool before lunch and Azziz served frozen daiquiris. Betty seemed as calm and as happy as she had been at dinner the night before.

'The day after tomorrow it's your birthday, Caroline. And I hope you'll be grateful to me for all the trouble and expense I've taken.' She said the words light-heartedly and smiled. 'In my opinion Dr Orville is certainly worth his fee.'

'Thank you,' Simon said.

Caroline stretched herself in the sun. 'And now, dear Mother, I'm going to take my psychiatrist back to my apartment and I shall make him lunch.'

Betty sighed. 'Well, I suppose it's all part of the treatment. Shall I see you both for dinner again?'

Simon glanced at Caroline.

'Maybe,' Caroline said. 'It's for my psychiatrist to decide.'

Betty raised her eyebrows enquiringly as they both left.

'I want you to sleep with me tonight,' Caroline said, when they reached the apartment.

'I can't wait,' Simon said. 'Let's forget about lunch.'

They made love and slept throughout the afternoon. Their bodies, warmed by the sun, increased their sensuality. Caroline whispered 'I'm glad I waited for you.'

Lying there on her bed with the yellow curtains pulled against the sunlight, which still filtered through and filled the room with an amber glow, Simon suddenly felt cold. At that moment he knew that he had thought of nothing all those hours because he dare not think any more, because he was more afraid than he had ever been in his life.

The intercom buzzed. It was Betty, Simon could hear her voice: 'I want to know if you're both dining with us tonight?' Betty asked.

Caroline's voice was cool. 'Dr Orville is,' she said. 'I shall dine alone.'

Simon looked at her as she replaced the 'phone. 'Why?' he said.

She shrugged. 'Because you're coming back here afterwards. I shall be with you all night. And I really can't stand that lot again.'

Simon bent over and kissed her. 'All right, I understand. I shall hurry over dinner and come straight to you.'

Caroline sighed. 'Besides, I want a few hours alone just to think about you. I'm very romantic, you know.'

Simon dressed and as he crossed the patio Sheila came to meet him, her face expressionless. 'Oh Dr Orville,' she said. 'There's someone on the telephone for you.'

'For me?' Simon asked.

Sheila turned to lead the way. 'You can take it in my office,' she said. He followed her into the house. She was walking quickly as if in a hurry.

Simon thought: who the hell can it be on the telephone. Suppose it was . . . his mind went blank. But he had to answer it; he must pick up that receiver and talk into it.

Sheila opened the door to her office, a small room with a desk neatly piled with papers, a silver tray with several pens, a bowl with paperclips, elastic bands, a cut glass vase filled with datura blossoms. And a white telephone. Its receiver lay on a piece of pink blotting paper. Sheila handed it to him.

'I'll leave you alone. It's probably private,' she said in her clipped tone.

Simon held the receiver, he heard Sheila's high heels echo on the tiled floor. She had reached the door. He could replace the receiver, then speak in the empty room. No one would know that he had not answered the call then.

He stood there, still holding the receiver, when Sheila paused; he heard her steps and half turned. She smiled at him. 'I forgot,' she murmured. 'Mrs Morrison wanted to see last month's accounts. She always thinks the servants are swindling her.' Sheila opened a drawer in the desk.

'Hello,' Simon said.

A voice spoke on the other end of the line. 'Is that Simon Perry?'

Simon clutched the receiver and the coldness spread through his body. The chill he had felt in Caroline's bed 10 minutes before now seemed to swell inside him and turn to ice.

'That is Simon Perry, I believe,' the voice was husky, dark, and Simon could not quite recognize it.

He pulled himself together. Sheila was still searching in a drawer. 'It's Dr Paul Orville,' he said.

'No. Dr Orville is dead. They found his corpse yesterday, pulled out from the Hotel Saada. One of the hotel waiters recognized him. So, what have you got to say about that, Simon Perry?'

Sheila left the room, he heard the door close. His mind was empty; he could think of nothing to say. But there was no need, for the voice continued. 'I'm contacting the police, they'll be at the villa very soon.'

'Why?' Simon said. 'I mean, why are you telling me?'

'Because I won't contact the police if you do exactly what I tell you to do now.'

'Tell me,' Simon said.

Chapter 14

He had obeyed the voice. As if he were sleepwalking he had
replaced the receiver and left the room. He had gone immediately to the garden gate and found it unlocked, as the voice had
said he would. He had opened the gate and slipped outside.
Nobody saw him leave. He wished then that both Simon Perry
and Dr Orville could vanish as easily.

Outside the villa a battered Chevrolet, covered in red dust,
stood waiting for him. The driver was the same deaf mute who
had driven him back from Mustapha, the night before last.

They drove quickly into Casablanca. Simon watched the sun
descend in the sky. He felt empty and desperate, nothing any
more seemed to matter. He might just as well watch this sun
which invested every outline with a golden haze, which turned
the stone walls into a warm tan and their shadows midnight blue;
he watched it as it slanted across the hills, softening them, slowly
smoothing them out so that they became part of the sky itself.

Then it was dark. And he could hear the traffic of Casablanca.
They turned off a main boulevard and the Chevrolet wound its
way through narrow streets, turning and twisting countless
times. Simon knew he would never find his way out again. He
felt utterly lost.

They stopped outside a large and crenellated building. The
deaf mute opened the car door and Simon stepped out. He faced
two wooden double doors, the sign against the evil eye was
painted on both sides. Someone opened the door and Simon
walked into a courtyard. A fountain sent its cooling spray over a
small pool filled with water lilies. The pool was surrounded by
shrubs of plumbago, all in flower so that everything seemed bril-
liantly blue.

The deaf mute pointed to a stone staircase and Simon ascended it. There was a gallery supported by columns which ran around three sides of the house. As he reached the top step, a door opened in front of him and Mustapha stood there.

'So glad you could come at such short notice, Mr Perry. Please come in.' Mustapha gestured to the interior of the room as he went on talking. 'I felt we should honour you tonight by giving you hospitality in my more elegant house. It struck me that the other night you may not have been impressed enough by your surroundings.'

Simon entered the room and heard the door shut softly behind him. Mustapha was right, the room was spacious, the walls were hung with rugs and tapestries, on a low table stood an earthenware pitcher of wine and around it were platters piled high with rice, meat and shellfish.

Clifton sat on a cushion by the table. Mustapha gently took Simon's arm and thrust him down next to Clifton.

'Our friend, Mr Perry, is not very talkative tonight, Clifton,' Mustapha said, pouring out three glasses of wine.

'Maybe he can only speak when he thinks he's a psychiatrist?' Clifton said with a grin.

'Why do you want to see me?' Simon asked.

'Drink, eat,' Mustapha said, with an expansive gesture of both hands to the table in front of them.

Simon felt hungry, he recalled he had eaten no lunch. He picked out a prawn from the platter, it was delicious. They ate with their right hands.

'You see,' Mustapha said. 'I am to be trusted. You come here and there are no police at the villa. Nor, if you do what we say will there be. But, alas, Mr Perry, you are not to be trusted. You agree with us the other night and then you return and you warn your patient. You bolt the gate, you even move stones in front of it. Well, it didn't surprise us, we thought you might go back on your word.'

Something caught Simon's eye over Mustapha's shoulder. A slight movement behind one of the tapestries. He went on eating the tiny spiced cubes of lamb, scooped up some rice flavoured with saffron, he listened to Mustapha and saw the movement again.

He had recognized Mustapha's voice, it had sounded deeper on the telephone.

Clifton took a gulp of red wine and wiped his mouth with his sleeve. 'Did you tell Mr Perry about the poor, dead Dr Orville?'

'Not all the details,' Mustapha smiled. 'It seemed that the doctor died only a few hours before they found him. For days they had heard knocking, you see, and at first a weak voice calling for help. What a dreadful death, Mr Perry. How Dr Orville must have suffered.'

Simon's arm trembled.

'Can you imagine, he was there for a week, slowly dying of thirst and hunger. Please eat, Mr Perry. Have you lost your appetite suddenly?'

'Stop it,' he begged. 'For pity's sake, stop it.'

'For an imposter and a thief you have a very soft heart, Mr Perry,' Mustapha continued. Then he clapped his hands. 'We will have some fruit.'

The tapestry moved. It seemed to swing suddenly outwards. Simon looked up. A servant wheeled a chair towards him. In the chair was a man. It was the same shape, the same huddled figure, and the eyes were staring at Simon. It was Dr Orville. And the chair was moving towards the table. Simon opened his mouth to scream, but no sound came. His terror seemed to have struck him as dead as the phantom itself.

The chair stopped.

Simon struggled to his feet. Mustapha was laughing. He stared down at Clifton. He was smoking kif and smiling happily. Did they know that a ghost was among them? The room began to swing around him. He was in the earthquake again, soon the house would crush them all, send them falling beneath the stones and pillars.

He heard Dr Orville's voice. 'What is happening? Tell me what is happening?'

It was the same cracked, hoarse voice Simon had heard before. He stared again at this apparition, forcing himself to look at it closely. The head was bandaged to hide the scar, but he saw wisps of white hair sticking out from the dirty bandages.

Simon stared at the chair, he saw that the bony wrists were tied to the arms of the chair, and then looking beyond he noticed that the tapestry had hidden a doorway onto the gallery outside and a servant now stood there holding a platter of fruit.

'He is alive,' Simon murmured, and sat down on the cushion.

Mustapha was still laughing. 'It was Clifton's idea to send you an apparition. He thought you had to be punished for not doing what you promised.'

'I was in your bathroom,' Clifton said, 'watching you. A touch of make-up had done wonders. It was worth every minute of it. Orville was so doped he didn't know where he was. Lovely touch that, when he begged you for help.'

Simon's head ached, but somewhere within him he felt a surge of relief. He might be a thief, but he wasn't a murderer. Dr Orville could not haunt him in nightmares any more. Then he glanced at the shrunken figure and felt a surge of compassion.

'Christ, what are you doing to him?' he asked.

For Dr Orville had indeed aged horribly since the night of the earthquake, his hair had gone white, his figure was emaciated, his skin scabrous and peeling.

Mustapha got up and pushed the chair nearer to Simon, then he leaned down and murmured in Dr Orville's ear.

'Dr Orville, meet Dr Orville,' Mustapha said.

The figure in the wheel-chair stared at Simon and gave a start. 'I don't understand,' he muttered in his hoarse voice.

'Then let me explain,' Clifton said to him. 'This man has taken your identity. He calls himself Dr Orville. He is being employed by Betty Morrison who wrote to you in Geneva. He has been giving treatment to her daughter, Caroline. In fact he is a plain imposter – a complete fraud.'

In his wheel-chair Dr Orville was still staring at Simon. 'You're the man I met in the bar at Agadir on the night of the earthquake,' he said slowly. 'I seldom forget a name, and you said your name was Simon Perry. Am I correct?'

Simon nodded.

Clifton laughed. 'Even when he was doped last night he recognized you. That's how we knew your name.'

Dr Orville glared at Simon. 'Then you are not only a crook, Simon Perry,' he said, 'but an idiot as well. How could you ever imagine that you could get away with it — even if I had been dead?'

'I was certain you were dead,' Simon answered. 'And in the hospital they thought I was Dr Orville because they discovered the card you gave me with your name and your Geneva address on it just before the earthquake. I had put it in my wallet with a few Moroccan banknotes. Though my trousers were torn, the wallet in my hip pocket was still intact. So I was identified as Dr Orville in the Casablanca hospital, and I took the chance. You must appreciate that I had seen part of the staircase fall and crush you. I tried to get through to you, but at that moment the ceiling fell on me, and I was buried. However, even though I'm not a psychiatrist, I have at least tried to help Caroline Morrison.'

'And a fine mess you've got us both into,' Dr Orville stated.

Simon thought under the circumstances this was a gross understatement. The doctor's body was so withered he seemed barely alive. Yet what was Dr Orville doing with Mustapha and Clifton?

'Whose side are you on?' Simon asked.

'I'm on any side that will expose your fraud,' Orville said, glowering at him.

Simon remembered the scandal in Geneva and he felt a sudden rush of anger. 'Well, what the hell are you doing here then?' he asked.

Orville hesitated.

'Why not tell him?' Clifton asked.

'I was one of the last to be dug out,' Dr Orville said slowly. 'I was put into a hospital near Agadir. I'd lost my medicine case which contained Mrs Morrison's address and telephone number. But I could still remember my own number. So when at last I reached Casablanca, I rang through to my secretary in Geneva, and she had the number of the villa. So I telephoned, and I got through to someone who I think must have been Mrs Morrison's secretary. I said that I was at the Hotel Excelsior in Casablanca. The secretary told me to stay where I was. I was informed that a car would be coming to my hotel to collect me within an hour. A car came with a Moroccan driver. I was brought to this villa.'

'From the fact that your wrists are tied to your wheel-chair, I would suppose that you are not staying here voluntarily,' Simon said.

'His wrists are bound to the chair to save him from falling,' Mustapha explained.

'That is their excuse,' Dr Orville said to Simon. 'But my wrists are unbound when I'm in the room they've given me. However, the door is then carefully locked from the outside. The truth is that I'm being held a prisoner.'

'We want to look after you,' Mustapha told him. 'We've already explained that you will be free to leave this house in 3 days' time.'

'After the examination of Caroline Morrison by the two doctors,' Dr Orville said, turning to Simon, 'I shall be released. I can walk with my crutches. I shall be given a large bribe and driven to the airport and put on a plane to Geneva. They make it sound so easy. And I'm sure their offer to you will sound equally simple. So why not accept the bribe they are certain to offer you? All you will be asked to do is to inject Caroline Morrison on the morning of the examination. You will use some hallucinatory drug I'm sure they have in their possession. It might be LSD. I'm equally sure that the bribe they offer you will be a large one, and since you're a crook you might as well accept it. Because I will have nothing to do with their scheme.'

Simon stared at him in distaste. His speech had not impressed him. 'You're making a great stance at being honest, Dr Orville. But what about the money you inherited? Wasn't there a scandal, a court inquest? Haven't Clifton and Mustapha tried to blackmail you about that?'

Dr Orville's skeletal hands gripped the arms of the wheel-chair. He stared at Simon as if he was a maniac. At the same time Clifton laughed.

'We've got nothing on the pure Dr Orville. That story was my idea.' Clifton glanced at Mustapha, who nodded. 'You see, this wreck of a psychiatrist, when he was pulled out of the earthquake, didn't even remember his own name . . . .'

'I couldn't remember. . . . At that time I couldn't remember,' Dr Orville murmured, shaking his head. 'But I knew I was a doctor.'

'But he had a kind of stupid pride,' Clifton continued, 'so he didn't admit in hospital that he'd forgotten almost everything. It was his secretary who first called him by his real name. Then bits of his old life returned to him. But whether he's dishonest or honest, in this state he's in he's not much use to us now is he? Half the time he's been here he's been delirious. We weren't sure then who was the real Dr Orville. So I cooked up that story the other night to see what effect it had on you. It was all pure fiction, but you believed in it, that's why we knew you were an imposter, so we thought a crook might play it our way. But you failed us, Mr Perry. And that won't do.'

Simon looked at the three of them and felt defiant. 'None of you understand,' he said. 'Even if Caroline takes some drug that morning and appears a raving lunatic, they have to prove that she's legally incompetent to manage the estate. It is not the same thing.'

'She is a raving lunatic,' Clifton said softly. 'And if they see that they're bound to think that she's legally incompetent.'

'I think you're the one that's mad,' Simon told Clifton. 'What the hell did you hope to do to me when you arranged for Dr Orville to appear in my room? And just now when he was pushed into here?'

Clifton laughed. 'We thought if we turned you into a gibbering idiot, at least then you could not harm our plans. It needed a certain amount of stage management.'

Suddenly Dr Orville spoke. 'They have all kinds of schemes,' he told Simon. 'You'll be offered a bribe, of course. And – as I've told you – since you're a crook you might as well accept it. But I will have nothing to do with their plans.'

Orville glared round the room defiantly. Mustapha spoke to

the Moroccan servant in Arabic. The man nodded. He took hold of the two handles at the back of the wheel-chair and pushed it slowly out of the room.

Chapter 15

There was silence.

'What's Mrs Morrison going to think when I haven't turned up at dinner? When I've vanished from her villa? Isn't she going to call the police?' Simon asked.

Mustapha folded his hands in his lap. 'That's been looked after.'

Clifton said 'You are a fool, Simon Perry. You've got three alternatives. We can expose you as a fraud, a criminal imposter and a thief, because we mustn't forget that you've stolen all the money that Orville had with him. If we called in the police you would be arrested immediately, and you would be sentenced to a long term of imprisonment. So we can expose you – or you can take the second alternative and accept a generous bribe from us.'

'What is the third alternative?' Simon asked.

'I believe Clifton mentioned that to you before,' Mustapha said. Mrs Morrison will find a corpse lying in the patio tomorrow morning. It is very simple.'

Simon nodded. He thought: I behaved like a crook by impersonating Orville, why not go the whole hog and accept this bribe they're offering? Caroline's life would not be ruined if she didn't inherit a fortune, and she would soon forget about him – or so he tried to persuade himself.

Simon realized that this was the moment when he would have to face up to the most profoundly moral question of his whole life. As he considered the alternatives, he remembered Orville's absurd understatement: 'And a fine mess you've got us both into.' Maybe it had been the same way all through his life. The dishonest part of him had always been a miserable failure. He had known that he had stolen the knife, yet he had been found using it by his form-master. On his plantation in Malaya he had accepted bribes so long as they could be considered gifts – and he had been politely paid off. It was like the doubtful deals; he was always the one who made least profit out of them. Moreover, Teena would not have come to live with him if he had not paid cash to her family. And now his most vital act of dishonesty seemed also to have failed. . . . Could the reason for his failures in dishonesty throughout his life spring from the fact that the honest side of him – certainly subconsciously – was far more powerful than the liar and the crook? During the last few days had he not suffered from guilt and nightmares because of his fraud? Perhaps in a way he was divided. If so, he must encourage the stronger side of his nature. His small acts of deceit together with this last attempt at complete fraud had brought him no happiness and had almost sent him mad.

At last, once and for all, Simon decided that he must change. He would make an effort to be honest and to remain honest. He felt as if he had been hiding the knife in his desk-drawer and had been caught with the theft. He was a poor kind of thief. But this decision came at a desperate moment. He knew he must now try to make good the wrong that he had done. Would there be an opportunity to do so? But his only hope of finding such a chance was to disguise his decision from Clifton and Mustapha. He needed time, and he must act accordingly. In their presence, he must constantly appear to be agreeing with their plans.

'I'm glad that you're taking time to consider the three alternatives,' Clifton said.

Simon looked at Clifton steadily. 'I'm sure you realize that there is only one possible decision for me to make,' he replied. 'But I hope you'll make my decision worthwhile. So my first question is this – how much?'

'Twenty thousand dollars,' Clifton said.

'How am I to know that I'll get paid?' Simon asked.

'Because you're in a strong position,' Clifton told him. 'We will have to tell you at least part of our plan, and once you know it you could report us to the police – just as we could report you to the police. We have to trust each other.'

'And what do I have to do?'

'You do nothing,' Clifton said. 'It's now one in the morning. We can easily get you back to the villa long before Betty wakes up.'

'But in her present state, are you sure that Caroline will be declared insane?' Simon asked, trying to sound casual.

'Not in her present state,' Mustapha said with a titter.

'Am I expected to dope her?' Simon asked.

'You're expected to do nothing,' Clifton replied. 'Just let events take their course when the doctors arrive. But don't interfere if you see anything unsual going on. And if Miss Caroline Morrison is declared legally incompetent there will be $20,000 for you. It's quite a high price for doing nothing.'

If Simon was to help Caroline he realized that his only chance was to discover their precise plans for making certain Caroline was declared legally incompetent.

'If I'm to do nothing, what's the point of bribing me?' Simon asked.

'The answer is simple,' Clifton replied. 'If when people wake up in the villa this morning, and your clothes are still in your bedroom, but you've disappeared, Betty will make a hell of a fuss. She's bound to ring the police, and we don't want the police around at the present moment.'

'What do you intend to do about Dr Orville?' Simon asked.

'The first thing we will do is to make certain that you hand back to Orville his Letter of Credit which we presume is in your possession,' Clifton said. 'You will pay him back the travellers' cheques he claimed must have been stolen. Then we will give him the cash that Betty would have given him if his cure had succeeded. And he can go happily back to Geneva and continue practising with his wretched drug.'

'I don't think that Orville is going to agree,' Simon said. 'His wrists were bound with bandages to the wheel-chair. And he didn't give me the impression of being very happy staying with you.'

'Because he doesn't trust us,' Clifton answered. 'He thinks that as soon as Caroline has been declared insane we'll just chuck him out. But we won't. As I told you, he'll get his own money back and the sum of money Betty would have paid him if his cure had succeeded. Remember, he hasn't met either Betty or Caroline, so he can have no loyalty to them.'

Mustapha got up from his chair and moved towards the door leading into the corridor. 'I must make sure that Orville is all right,' Mustapha said. Simon did not believe it, he was sure Mustapha would feel no concern for anyone. He left the room. Clifton and Simon were alone together. Clifton took up a pipe with a long stem and a small bowl and began to smoke. Gradually, the smell of kif filled the room.

'You must think that I'm a cold-blooded crook,' Clifton said to Simon.

'Not necessarily,' Simon replied.

'I'm determined you should understand my point of view,' Clifton said. 'I want you to be on my side. You must appreciate the reason for my actions. You see, when I was a child I had a very sheltered life at home. I wanted to love my father, but he didn't have any time for me. He didn't bully me, yet he always kept a tight control over me – even when I was growing up. But when I got out to Korea I met every type of person you can imagine. I came to understand how confined and how stupid were the values of the people I knew back home. In Korea I mixed with a group of young people of my own age who had a completely different set of values. They believed in living life to the full – even if that meant taking the risk of being discovered by the authorities concerned. On the surface, we must have seemed very irresponsible. When we got the chance we smoked, we took drugs, we filled the brothels. But beneath all this illegal behaviour there was a serious purpose. We wanted to try to discover what the point was in life. So we examined various religions and various philosophies. It's hard to explain. But I, for one, began to see a faint ray of light at the end of the tunnel. Then I was invalided home and I went back to live in my father's apartment in New York. My mother was dead, but my father led much the same life as he had done before his two marriages. He was a staunch Republican who demanded respectability – according to his code –

from the people around him. I tried to persuade him to give me money to have a pad of my own, but he wouldn't – because in his formal way he was fond of me, even though he disapproved of me. There was no persuading him. He just couldn't understand. So I had to lead a secret life. Then I was arrested for being in possession of marijuana – quite a large quantity. My father was appalled and disgusted, but he did what he could to help me. It was a terrible thing for his son to be arrested.

'When I came back home he told me I must give up the life I had been leading and take a responsible job in his firm. I refused. We had the most terrible row. My father shouted at me in his rage. I couldn't bear it any longer. I told him I would never live under the same roof with him again and would rather live in the gutter than in his grandiose but stuffy apartment. My father was trembling with anger. I went to my room to pack my clothes. Then I returned to say goodbye to him. He was calmer, but still very bitter. He told me that as far as he was concerned I was no son of his. He gave me a cheque for $25,000 and said he never wanted to see me again.

My family's friends thought I had gone back to the Far East, but I was, in fact, here in Morocco. I heard later that my father was sorry he had thrown me out. He wanted to see me again. But no-one had any address for me. He even employed a detective agency. But I had left America without leaving a trace behind me. No-one knew I was in Morocco. I used a different name. Then I read in an American newspaper that my father had had a stroke and died.

'I wondered if I should get in touch with my father's lawyers. But I was afraid of getting tied up in the life from which I had escaped. I wanted real freedom. In this country I've found it. But it costs money. That's where Mustapha comes in. I met him at a casual party in Tangier where he was living. He was a great help. He could tell you where to get a loaf of bread or a wallet of kif cheaper than anywhere else. We have remained friends. And just recently he has been of tremendous value. . . . I'm telling you all this because I want you to appreciate my side of the case. When my father tried to get in touch with me I'm sure that if I'd gone back to see him in New York we could have worked out some way of living in the same town and meeting frequently. And I probably would have inherited half his fortune, and Caroline would have inherited the rest. But now, as it is, if the doctors decide that Caroline is sane I shall get nothing. Not a cent – according to the family lawyers who I've consulted because I was running short of cash. And the cost of the bare necessities of life are rising here in Morocco – just as they are everywhere else. Are you beginning to see my point of view? Under the terms of the Will, if Caroline is found insane I inherit the whole property. I wish I could have come to some agreement with Caroline to split the fortune. But Betty would never let me anywhere near her. And now it's too late. And I'm almost broke. So do you blame me for wanting to make sure that Caroline is proved insane? Betty took the first dishonest step by writing to Dr Orville in Geneva. If Betty had been convinced that Caroline was sane, would she have sent for a psychiatrist from Switzerland? I can see Betty's plan quite clearly. She wants Caroline to be declared sane, but wants her sanity to last only for a brief period. She doesn't care a rap for Caroline's welfare. She wants her to relapse into the state Caroline has been in since she was a young girl, so that she is totally dependent on Betty, and Betty will be in control of the money. Now do you understand?'

'I am beginning to see your point of view,' Simon said to Clifton. 'And I do think that the Will was unfair. But tell me this. Who arranged for the nightly visits of the little Moroccan girl?'

'Why do you want to know?' Clifton enquired.

'Because if you want me to go back to the villa, I've got to know who is on your side and who is against you.'

'If we thought it was important we would tell you. And why should you care?' Clifton asked. 'All you have to do is carry on as if nothing had happened and continue with your pretence of being a psychiatrist. No one is going to get in your way, I promise you.'

'But I must know the truth,' Simon told him. 'I presume it was Mustapha who got hold of the young Moroccan girl?'

Clifton re-filled his pipe. 'Perhaps,' he answered.

'And who answered the telephone at the villa when Dr Orville rang up? I presume it must have been Sheila Adams.'

'Possibly,' Clifton replied. 'You may guess who our agent is in the villa, but I warn you that there is nothing you can do about it. You've got no proof that the person has done anything wrong. So just let things be, and you'll get your money.'

'I have another question,' Simon said. 'How did Mustapha get hold of Sheila?'

'I should have thought you could work out that one for yourself,' Clifton replied. 'I'm sure you will in time, so I might as well tell you now. In the days before Independence, the International Zone flourished. Tangier was the most popular meeting place for tourists and for crooks. I managed to avoid meeting Betty and Caroline. Mustapha was my source of information. Betty met Sheila in a café in Tangier. Sheila was in a completely drunken state because the Moroccan she was living with at the time was Mustapha, and earlier that evening they had had a violent row. For some reason, Betty was sorry for Sheila and decided to take her on as her secretary. When Sheila returned to the little flat she shared with Mustapha just off the Zocco Chico, she told him of Betty's offer, and Mustapha immediately saw our opportunity. He told Sheila to accept the job. He moved to Casablanca when Betty did, and he bought this house. Sheila was now Betty's secretary so Mustapha knew exactly what was going on at the villa and could act accordingly. Of course he kept in close touch with me, and recently I joined him in Casablanca.'

'And how about Dr Orville?' Simon asked. 'How does he fit in with your plans?'

'So far as Dr Orville is concerned, if our plan is to work smoothly it is essential that he does not cause any trouble. And this is where you can help.'

'Why should I?' Simon asked.

'You surprise me,' Clifton said. 'I thought you understood your position. I hate to have to remind you that if Orville or one of us exposed you, then you would be put in prison. You've made the wise choice by accepting a bribe from us. All I am asking you now is to go and calm Orville. Tell him he's going to get paid.

Tell him he's going to get his money back. Tell him that he doesn't need to worry about Caroline. Nothing terrible is going to happen to her. Tell him I'm keeping him here to make sure that he doesn't telephone the police or get hold of some drug to make Caroline appear to be sane for at least a few hours. As soon as the doctors have gone, I'll put Orville on a plane to Geneva. Remember that Orville isn't in all that strong a position. He wasn't being paid by Betty to administer aspirins to the girl. I want you to try to make Orville see reason. We must make absolutely certain that he doesn't contact the police as soon as we let him go.'

'I'm surprised you should trust me alone with Orville,' Simon answered. 'He is the only proof you've got that I'm a fake. How do you know that I wouldn't arrange for Orville to have an "unfortunate accident"?'

Clifton had begun to play with his beads, running them up and down the string which held them together. 'You know if you did harm Orville you'd never get out of this villa,' Clifton said. 'I have a conscience of sorts, but I can assure you that Mustapha is more ruthless than I am. I saw him in a fight at a bar in Tangier. And I realized that at heart he is a killer. I saw it all. If you were to see him with one of his little girls I'm afraid you'd find it disgusting.'

'But the stripes were painted,' Simon said.

'There were girls he could have produced for you where the scars would have been real. But he wanted the same girl to appear on each occasion.'

'You approve of all this?' Simon asked.

Clifton stopped clicking his beads. He held up the string so that they all clustered at one end of it. 'I don't approve of Mustapha or his habits,' Clifton answered. 'Unfortunately, in the world in which I live, people like Mustapha are essential to me.'

'Isn't that the kind of remark your father would have made when he was confronted with a rival business firm?'

'I don't know,' Clifton answered impatiently. 'And I don't care. I was never allowed to find out what went on behind the scenes. But that doesn't concern you. At the present moment you must realize that we could put the police on to you. Be reasonable. All we want is for you to try and make Orville see the form. He's a phoney psychiatrist. He's been hired to do a phoney job. He's now going to get paid for not doing the job. So what has he to complain about?'

'I see your point,' Simon replied. 'But I doubt if Orville will.'

'Try it and find out,' Clifton told him, glancing at his watch. 'There's plenty of time.'

'There's another thing,' Simon said, staring hard at Clifton. 'Did Betty ever try and seduce you?'

Clifton dropped the beads. 'That old bag? She guarded my father's purse strings like the Bank of England. She always hated me and turned my father against me.'

'Did you ever go to the house in Connecticut?'

'Yeah. One summer.'

'When Caroline was fourteen?'

'She was about that age.'

'Why?'

'To try and get Betty to use her influence on my father. But she damn well wouldn't.' Clifton got up from the cushion. 'Now I'll take you to Orville's room and leave you there. I shan't lock the door, but I'll come and tell you when it's time to leave.'

Chapter 16

Clifton led Simon down a narrow passage and opened a door at the far end. The room was small and badly furnished. There were bars on the window. Orville was lying in bed. He was wearing pyjamas of a violent red colour which probably belonged to Mustapha. Orville's two crutches lay beside his bed. He was propped up by pillows. He looked very weak, yet his eyes were still bright. For a moment there was silence. Orville was glaring at the two of them.

'I've brought along Simon Perry,' Clifton told Orville. 'He wants to talk to you. If you need me I'll be in the living-room.'

Clifton turned and left the room. They could hear him walking down the passage. Orville broke the silence. 'I would never have thought that you were a crook,' he said to Simon.

'Nor did I most of the time,' Simon answered. 'But when I was in hospital I was given the opportunity. They were convinced I was Dr Orville because they had found your card in my wallet. I couldn't resist the chance. But I must tell you that I haven't touched the Letter of Credit, and I've spent £500 of your £3,000 in travellers' cheques. I might as well add – though I don't expect you to believe me – that I did try to rescue you in the Hotel Saada before I was buried alive.'

'Why did Clifton bring you to see me?' Orville asked.

'Because he wants you to be realistic,' Simon answered.

'You mean he wants me to trust in the promises he and Mustapha have made me. He wants me to believe you will give me back my money and I will be paid as if I had cured Caroline Morrison.'

'Exactly.'

'And do you believe it?' Orville asked.

'I'll give you back the money I've got of yours,' Simon told

124

him. 'You can believe that.'

'Why should I believe a crook?' Orville asked.

'Perhaps I'm not as real a crook as part of me would like to be. Perhaps at heart I'm honest. Whatever drugs you may use you are at least a trained psychiatrist. So you must be able to analyse me and know if I'm telling the truth. But I'm beginning to believe that all of us have a streak of dishonesty in us. For instance, you, Dr Orville, have a slight streak of dishonesty in you – otherwise you wouldn't have accepted Betty's offer. After all, you must have known that a psychiatrist may spend weeks or months or years giving consideration to the problems of his patient. From Betty's letters you must have realized that Caroline was a difficult case. But you trusted in your drug to do the trick for a while at least. But at the end of that period you must have appreciated that Caroline might need prolonged treatment. However, by then you would have flown back to Geneva.'

'And Caroline Morrison would have inherited the money and have been in a position to find herself the best doctors and the best treatment in the world,' Dr Orville pointed out.

'But would she have done so?' Simon asked. 'How can we tell? Supposing there hadn't been an earthquake, supposing you hadn't been intercepted, supposing you had gone to Betty's villa, what was *your* game? What were you going to do with your "wonder drug"? I've told you. Temporarily at least – that is for the time of the doctors' examination of the girl, you were going to pretend you had cured her. But you must have known from her case history that she was only mildly hysterical and would have passed any test.'

'You're wrong,' Orville replied. 'Caroline Morrison had hallucinations. She still has – and you know it because I gather you've seen her for quite a time. My "wonder drug", as you call it, could have restored her.'

'What is this drug of yours?' Simon asked. 'Or is it a secret?'

'It's a secret, but I can tell you its basis is Largactil – the trade name for chlorpromazine. Most drugs have two names – the chemical and the trade name. My so-called "wonder-drug" is a derivative of Largactil. It's like making a cocktail. For instance you can start with a basis of gin, and then you can add something to give it flavour. Drugs are mixed in a similar way.' He seemed to come alive as he explained about his drug, as if it was his only child that he was devoted to.

'How long have you been using the drug?' Simon asked.

'For several years,' Dr Orville answered. 'And I've found it particularly effective for patients who suffer from hallucinations.'

'The only hallucination Caroline has – so far as I know – is that almost every night a young Moroccan girl appears on her balcony, pulls apart her robe, and shows that she has been savagely whipped. But let me tell you that the Moroccan girl is no hallucination. I've caught hold of her. I've torn apart her robe, and the lash marks are painted on her back.'

'So what do you intend to do?' Orville asked.

'Do you think they've got a mike hidden somewhere?' Simon asked.

'I doubt it,' Orville answered. 'They could hardly have foreseen that the two of us would be in this room alone together.'

Simon nodded but still lowered his voice. 'They are taking me back to the villa,' he told Orville, 'because they think that if I disappeared Betty would call in the police. So I'm going back. I've convinced Caroline that the Moroccan girl wasn't a hallucination. And I'll do all I can to help Caroline because I'm now fond of her, and I'm certain that she is sane – inasmuch as any of us are sane. When that's all over I'm not quite sure what I shall do, but I'm determined to help Caroline.'

'You'll be lucky if you get away with it,' Orville told him. 'You might find it simpler to be dishonest.'

'I don't think so,' Simon answered.

'You mentioned just now that you thought there was a streak of dishonesty in all of us,' Orville said. 'It may well be that there is also a streak of insanity in us. And the dividing line between the two conditions may at times be very thin.' Simon looked at the exhausted man on the bed and was intrigued to hear the phrase he had thought of the night before. 'In the days when I was practising, if I certified a man insane it was because I

126

believed that his mind was unsound. I believed he might be a danger to himself and others and needed treatment in a mental hospital. But at the very second I certified the man, I was aware that there were many others who were considered to be sane but whose minds were completely unsound. In the case of Caroline Morrison you will appreciate that I have only been able to judge her case by second-hand evidence. You now tell me that the Moroccan girl was a fake hallucination. But there is another aspect of the case which I'm sure any expert in the field would find disturbing to say the least – and that is her desire for isolation. In my profession it has been discovered that complete isolation is as dangerous as physical starvation. The trouble is that most of us have been brought up to believe that there is something splendid and admirable – even saint-like – in isolation and complete independence from other people. But there have been philosophers and writers throughout the ages who have told us the opposite. The English poet and philosopher, John Donne, puts it perfectly. I quote from memory. "No man is an island, entire of itself; every man is a piece of the continent, a part of the main." And if, as an alienist, I were to examine Caroline Morrison the first thing I would observe would be the complete isolation in which I gather she lives.'

'Do you believe what you are saying?' Simon asked. 'Or are you saying it to disguise the thin streak of dishonesty which made you come to Morocco?'

Orville gazed at Simon for a while. 'How can I tell?' he asked.

'Look,' Simon said very quietly, 'this seems to have developed into an enquiry about our beliefs. I'm convinced there's a streak of dishonesty in all of us. From your attitude and from what you say I gather there is also a streak of madness in all of us. Right. I think you're probably correct. But we haven't yet settled our attitude. Do we tolerate these streaks of dishonesty and madness in ourselves or do we condemn them? I've made my decision. Have you, Dr Orville, in all sincerity made yours?'

'For a confessed crook, you are very confident,' Orville said.

'Only because I've made my decision,' Simon answered.

'But all the reasoning in the world isn't going to help you or me in our present state. So what do you intend to do?'

'I'm going back to the villa,' Simon said. 'I shall do all I can to help Caroline. Can you please give me an answer to a question?'

'It depends what the question is,' Orville answered.

'When you telephoned the villa, was it a woman who answered the telephone?'

'Yes.'

'English?'

'I would say so. . . . From her conversation I imagined she was some kind of secretary. She seemed extremely interested when I assured her I was indeed Dr Orville and I had been one of the last people to be dug out of the ruins of the Hotel Saada. I feel sure that the woman must have been Mrs Morrison's secretary.'

'You're right,' Simon told him. 'Her name is Sheila Adams, and she is a secretary. . . . Now can you tell me something else? It's something technical. If you were using an electric fruit extractor to make orange juice, could you put some powder into the drink so it couldn't be detected?'

'Why are you treating me as if I were on your side?' Dr Orville asked suddenly.

'Because I think you *are* on my side – whether you like it or not,' Simon answered. 'I reckon that the streaks of dishonesty or madness in you are so thin as to be almost unrecognisable. So I repeat. Could some drug in liquid or powder form be put into the drink?'

'Easily,' Orville replied. 'Even by a Moroccan servant. Besides, Moroccans are expert at drugs of this kind.'

'It seems that the Fatima can't work the machine, so Sheila, the secretary, does it for her, and I believe she could mix something in it. I mean some hallucinatory drug such as LSD.'

'That's correct,' Dr Orville murmured.

'What drug did they give you last night when you appeared in my room at the villa?' Simon asked.

Orville shook his head. 'I remember they drove me somewhere, but I've been given heavy doses of morphine for the pain, I don't know what else. Sometimes, as now, my mind is clear. At other times, there are just shapes, smells . . . half-remembered, like some terrible dream. An angry man holding a lighted candelabra.' Orville closed his eyes. 'Images like that,' he murmured.

Simon looked at the thin shape beneath the sheet and felt real compassion. 'I'm sorry,' he said. 'You've been through a terrible experience and now it is continuing. Christ, I wish I could get you out of here into a hospital.' He paused. 'Are they feeding you properly?'

Orville opened his eyes. 'There's not much I can keep down, to tell you the truth. They don't seem good on making wholesome broth.' He smiled weakly at Simon.

'It's my fault. I swear to you that I shall make it up to you.' Simon went to the bed and picked up Orville's hand. 'You must believe me. I can't endure seeing you in this state,' Simon dropped the hand and stared down at him.

Orville leaned forward in bed and examined Simon's face carefully. 'Supposing I believe you,' Orville said after a pause. 'Supposing I were to help you. What could I do?'

'Not much at present,' Simon answered. 'Just tell Clifton and Mustapha that you're thinking over the proposals they've made to you. As soon as I get back to the villa I shall warn Caroline again. I shall also tell her the whole truth about myself.'

'Will you warn Mrs Morrison of their plot?' Orville asked.

'No,' Simon replied. 'I can't trust Betty because she drinks too much and could get hysterical. And remember – so far as Clifton and Mustapha are concerned – that you must continue to believe that I am a crook. Don't ask me to do anything for you from the outside even though I want to. Because that won't help Caroline, and at this moment I can't put my head in their noose. You will have to wait until Caroline has been declared legally competent and I have got out of this country. By that time you will have been released, and you can expose me if you want. That I can promise you. But don't trust either of them for any bribes. Just try and be thankful that you were hauled out of that earthquake and have most probably escaped the ruin of your reputation by a couple of crooks.'

'At the moment I've got no choice,' Orville whispered sourly.

'Surely it's a question of intention,' Simon replied. He knew he was being harsh in his manner but he had no choice if he was to save them all. 'What do you want to get out of it all? Be sensible. Admit to yourself that your mission has failed. Be grateful that you're still alive.'

'It's not easy to be grateful when you're in my position,' Orville said bitterly. 'We have spoken about streaks of dishonesty. What about the two specialists who are flying over from New York to diagnose Caroline Morrison's condition? What about their streak of dishonesty in persuading themselves that they can determine the girl's state of mind in the course of a day's examination? They can't. When I heard about them from Mrs Morrison I realised that however expert the two of them might be they could not attest the girl's mental state in such a short time. But I'm sure they will turn out to be honest and so established in their profession that each of them would ignore any bribe that was offered him by either side. Yet they must know – or at least in their hearts they must know – that their mission is specious. And that is where their streak of dishonesty enters in – because obviously, under the terms of the Will, a considerable allowance in cash must have been made for the two doctors who presumably have been chosen by the late Mr Henry Morrison's lawyers.'

Orville lay back against the pillows. 'In your newly-found honesty,' he said, 'when you are with Caroline, tell me this. Does she display any violent and unreasonable dislike of any person?'

'No,' Simon replied. 'But her relationship with her mother is a difficult one. At times Mrs Morrison shows real concern and affection for Caroline, at other times she quite obviously resents her with an emotion akin to hatred.'

Dr Orville nodded. 'And what about Caroline?'

'The same really. She admits to a love-hate relationship with her mother.'

'Not at all uncommon with children and parents,' Dr Orville said dryly. 'But how violent is that feeling?'

Simon paused. 'It's difficult for me to tell.'

'Naturally,' Dr Orville looked pleased for the first time that evening. 'You are not a trained psychiatrist.'

'We all have violent emotions,' Simon said lamely.

'Yes. But it is when they become self-destructive, when the hatred for a parent consumes the patient so entirely that the patient no longer sees the real parent, but a symbolic castrator. A God-figure who can create or destroy their own life.' Dr Orville paused. 'Now tell me, what are Miss Morrison's feelings about her dead father?'

'She loved him very much. More perhaps, utter devotion. She was plunged into misery when he died.' Simon looked at the doctor who nodded quietly to himself as if the pattern fitted.

'Jealousy,' he murmured. 'The mother and the daughter vying for the love and affection of the father. It is very common. Most families in some degree or another have elements and variations upon the Oedipal theme. Most of us suppress them entirely, are not even conscious that they exist, and that they are the prime movers in our adult psychology. We tend to repeat the pattern in our marriages and our relationships, seeking in our partner either the security we had from a parent, or in other cases, the elements that were missing from our parental upbringing.'

'How does this help me to understand and help Caroline?' Simon asked.

'It doesn't,' Dr Orville said crisply, 'because as I said before, you're not trained.'

Simon thought that this discussion appeared to be giving the doctor back some strength and authority.

'Now, what about paranoia?' The doctor continued. 'Does Miss Morrison feel she is persecuted by anyone or anything?'

Simon nodded. 'Yes, she does. She feels that someone is plotting against her. And we've discovered this is true. So, I hardly think that that is proof of any mental instability.'

'Did she ever feel paranoiac about her mother?'

Simon hesitated. 'No, I don't think so.'

'You don't seem very sure.'

There was a pause, then Simon said, 'As you say, I'm not really in a trained position to judge.'

The doctor smiled again. 'From what you tell me I think Mrs Morrison is the main source of Caroline's troubles. She is the victim of a hysterical and possessive mother. She is also the victim of all of those who for one reason or another wish her to be declared insane. If only we could arrange for her to be removed from her present environment she might become as normal a person as any one of us.'

As Orville spoke they could hear footsteps in the passage. The door opened and Clifton came in.

'I think it's time for Mustapha to drive you back to the villa,' he said to Simon. 'Have you had a satisfactory session with Dr Orville?'

'I believe so,' Simon answered.

'I'm thinking over the proposals you have made to me,' Orville told Clifton.

Immediately Simon realized there was a chance that his conversation with Orville had had some effect.

'I hope you will find the proposals satisfactory,' Clifton replied. 'But now Simon must leave you. And I think you ought to get some sleep. Ring when you want breakfast.'

'Goodbye, Dr Orville,' Simon said.

'Goodbye to you,' Orville answered in an expressionless voice. He leaned back on the pillows and closed his eyes.

Chapter 17

It was obvious to Simon that they still did not trust him, for the deaf mute Moroccan was nowhere to be seen. It was Mustapha who led him out of the villa and to the car outside. Mustapha drove the battered Chevrolet fast but well. Simon glanced at his wrist watch and saw that it was five in the morning. Dawn was beginning to break when they reached the open plain. Simon glanced at Mustapha. His eyes were fixed on the road. Had it not been for Caroline, Simon thought, this would be the moment to try to escape. But he had promised Caroline he would stay at the villa as long as she needed him, and now, for emotional reasons, he could not leave her.

'What are you going to do when this is over?' Mustapha asked suddenly.

Simon thought quickly. Neither Mustapha nor Clifton could know of the passage he had booked to Vera Cruz. His ticket was in his suitcase which was carefully locked. It had a complicated lock, and the keys were in his pocket. He doubted whether Sheila could open the case.

'What will you do?' Mustapha repeated.

'I haven't decided,' Simon told him.

'Remember you will have left the villa, and you will be a free agent,' Mustapha said. 'What will you do with the $20,000 we will be giving you?'

'I haven't thought,' Simon answered. 'It's certainly an exciting prospect.'

Mustapha tittered. 'Think of the number of girls you can buy,' he said. 'Girls or boys – whichever you prefer. But I think you prefer the girls.'

'I do,' Simon replied.

'So do I,' Mustapha told him.

Simon glanced at him. With his well-shaped lean face and his smooth bronze skin, Mustapha must be extremely attractive to women, Simon decided. Mustapha had taken off his *djellaba*; he was wearing a blue cashmere sweater and tight-fitting blue trousers; his clothes revealed his broad shoulders and slim waist. Any woman looking at him was sure to admire the charm of his face and the promise of virility displayed by his lithe and sinuous build.

'But I'm not interested in a girl when she's fully grown,' Mustapha continued. 'As Clifton may have told you, I only like the little ones.'

Simon wanted to get as much information as he could from Mustapha, so he made up his mind that however much he disliked the man he must try to flatter him. At that moment a small dog ran across the road. Mustapha did not alter his speed, and he kept the car on a steady course. There was a yelp and a bump as the car drove over the dog. Mustapha smiled, and turned his head for a moment and looked at Simon.

'You seem shocked,' he said.

'I am,' Simon could not help replying. 'Very shocked.' Mustapha stared at the road ahead. His face was distorted with temper.

'This is what would have happened if I had tried to avoid killing the dog,' he said. Then violently, he put on the brakes.

The car lurched, ran onto the verge, and seemed as if it would fall into the ditch, but Mustapha turned the wheel adroitly until they were on the road again.

'What is the life of an animal worth?' Mustapha asked. 'The papers say that in England you beat your children to death. If we kill a dog, what have you got to complain about? In your mind you accuse me of killing a dog, because you English care for your animals very much, yet you will allow your children to be beaten horribly.'

Simon could feel anger rising in him, as he remembered what Clifton had said about Mustapha's treatment of young girls. But he controlled himself, for he knew he must not say anything to antagonize Mustapha.

'It was clever of you to think up the idea of the little Moroccan girl on the balcony,' Simon told him after a pause.

The grim look disappeared from Mustapha's face.

'The plan was working perfectly until you came along,' he said. 'I trained the girl well. . . . I chose a girl because I am not at all interested in men or boys. I was never like Toni in those days. And if you are interested I can tell you why.'

Simon nodded. 'I'm most interested,' he replied.

'When I was 13,' Mustapha continued, 'an older boy who was big for his age asked me to his room. He gave me some little cakes to eat. In them he had mixed some *majoun* – a kind of kif. I ate three of them. I felt dizzy. He put me on his bed and raped me. I woke up in pain. I escaped from his room. I was in pain for a long time, and I had to go and see a doctor. I have never been to bed with a boy or a man since that evening. But I soon found that there were women who liked going to bed with me and would pay for it.'

Wryly Simon remembered Dr Orville's statement in the bar: 'If you tell people that you are a psychiatrist they begin to pour out all their troubles, their whole damned life history.' And Simon was not even a genuine practitioner, as Mustapha must know. Perhaps in every person there was an instinct to communicate his problems to a willing listener. Or perhaps there was something in Simon's nature which encouraged people to confide in him.

'When I was 17,' Mustapha was saying, 'there was an English woman who was very much in love with me. She was married and about fifty. I would go and visit her every afternoon when her husband was out at his office, and she paid me a lot of money.'

Simon looked at Mustapha once again. There was a sly look on his smooth brown face. It was easy to imagine the effect of his attractions on a middle-aged woman whose husband, perhaps, was no longer virile. 'Is that how you learned to speak English?' Simon asked.

'More or less,' Mustapha answered. 'But then it occurred to me that if I could make that much money out of my women, so could other boys with other women of about the same age as she was. So I chose a few boys who would do anything for cash, and I set up as a masseur. The ladies could come and choose what masseur they wanted. All the boys were willing. I met Toni during those days, but we never got on well together. My business went well. Then I met Sheila, and she came to live with me in the Zocco Chico.'

'How long have you known Sheila?' Simon asked.

'I have known Sheila since those days when I was in Tangier,' Mustapha replied. 'She was mad for me. She would do anything I asked. The trouble was that she was too demanding. And I have told you my tastes. But she would do what I ordered her to do. It was I who persuaded her to take on the job with Betty Morrison. Her acceptance of the job had two advantages. The first was that I need only see her once a week to satisfy her. The second was that she could give me information about the villa.'

'Did you know about Caroline and the Will in those days?' Simon asked.

'I knew that Betty Morrison had an attractive daughter who was reputed to be an heiress. But it was Betty who interested me,' Mustapha said. 'She still had some money left, and I was told she was very generous with the men who were her lovers. Particularly if they were good lovers. And I can be a very good lover when I try. But then Tariq ben Kassim – or Toni as he is called – appeared on the scene and spoiled my chances. So far as I know he was the first man that she really wanted to live with her. Perhaps it was because he was a good lover, or perhaps it was because he never asked her for any money – which was very clever of him, because he got more that way.'

'Sheila must be very useful in your latest plan for Caroline.'

'Very,' Mustapha replied.

'Did Sheila sometimes put drugs in the orange juice she made for Caroline?'

'You ask too many questions,' Mustapha answered.

'But I thought I was going to be let in on your plans,' Simon said.

'Not all of them,' Mustapha replied. 'We still need proof that you are on our side.'

'So Sheila has been told to spy on me?' Simon asked.

'Yes,' Mustapha answered. 'She has. And now that you have been warned, there is one question I would like you to answer me. Why did you spend so much time with Caroline in her apartment?'

'You must remember that I was acting the part of Dr Orville,' Simon replied. 'I had to spend some time with her.'

'Do you find her attractive?'

'Caroline is a very beautiful girl, as you know,' Simon said. 'But she's very highly strung and unstable.'

'You were afraid to make love to her?'

'Certainly, because if she had resented it, I would have been thrown out.'

'You were afraid to take the risk?'

'Yes.'

'But the girl seems to have disliked all the other doctors Betty has called in to examine her,' Mustapha said. 'Why did she allow you to stay in her room so long?'

'I simply don't know,' Simon answered.

They were now approaching the winding road that led up the hill to the villa. Mustapha turned left into the lane that was almost completely concealed from view by mimosa trees. Slowly the car moved along a rough track until through the bushes Simon could see the crenellated walls of the villa. Mustapha stopped the car outside the small door in the wall.

'This is where we part,' Mustapha announced. He got out of the car and produced a key from his pocket with which he opened the door.

Mustapha held open the door for Simon. 'Remember what you have been told to do,' Mustapha said softly. 'Just let events take their course, and don't interfere in anything. Remember you are still Dr Orville so far as the people in the villa are concerned.'

'With the exception of Sheila,' Simon added.

'Yes,' Mustapha replied. 'With the exception of Sheila'.

Mustapha gestured Simon to go through the door. 'Do not

forget what I have told you to do,' he said. 'And now good night.'

Mustapha closed the door behind him. Simon could hear the key being turned in the lock and a moment later the sound of the car driving away. He walked across the garden towards the villa. He glanced at his watch. The time was now 7 o'clock.

The fronds of the palm trees were clicking in a gentle breeze. The sun was filtering through the trees. Simon had had no sleep all night, but for once he did not feel tired. He turned the handle of the back door of the villa and walked along the corridor. Suddenly the door of the living-room opened and Sheila appeared. She was wearing a purple dressing gown; she looked less calm than usual. But her face was already made up, and her scarlet-painted toe-nails protruded from white sandals.

'I heard the car,' she told Simon, 'so I thought I would greet you on your return from Casablanca. Luckily the night watchman is asleep.'

'Have you been awake all night?' Simon asked as he followed her into the living-room.

'Mustapha telephoned me,' Sheila said. 'The 'phone only rings in my room at night because the others hate being disturbed. But I now know the form about you. I know that you are a fake and a complete crook. I know you would be put in prison if Mustapha informed the police.'

'Mustapha told you?' Simon asked.

'He spoke for quite a time. I must confess I wasn't at all surprised.'

'Because the real Dr Orville had telephoned you when he reached Casablanca?' Simon said.

'He had indeed,' Sheila replied.

'Now that you know I'm a fake, what are you going to do about it?'

'I've been told to do nothing for the time being,' Sheila answered.

'You obey your orders?' Simon asked.

'Yes,' Sheila replied. 'And I hope you will remember yours.' She paused. 'By the way, I told Betty that you were dining with Caroline last night. She looked quite jealous.'

138

Simon ignored Sheila's relish at this reaction of Betty's for he was determined to find out how much Mustapha had told Sheila. '*What* are my orders?' Simon asked.

'Don't prevaricate,' Sheila said. 'Mustapha assured me they were very clear.'

'What orders?' Simon asked once again.

'For one thing – not to interfere with anything I am to do. For another – to continue with your role as Dr Orville.'

'Why do you do it?' Simon asked.

'Do what?'

'Why do you side with Mustapha and Clifton?'

Sheila stared at him angrily. 'That's none of your business,' she said.

'But it *is* my business,' Simon answered. 'I want to make sure that you're going to be reliable. After all, think of the risk you are taking. Here you are, living in comfort in a large villa, and you're very well paid I'm sure. And your work can't be very arduous. You are living in ease and luxury. Why risk it all?'

Sheila's face was flushed with anger as she glared at Simon. 'What a fool you are!' she said. 'An idiot, in fact. You talk of ease and luxury. But you've met Betty. You must know what she's like. Well, think of the life I lead, being at her beck and call constantly. Having to listen over and over again to her boring stories about the celebrities she's met. Having to listen to her silly jokes and laugh at them. Having to fetch her a cigarette box when she's only got to stretch out her hand for it. Can't you see? I'm no better than a slave here.'

'Then why do you stay?' Simon asked.

Sheila's eyes darkened with hatred. 'But I'm not staying here,' she answered. 'That's the whole point. That's why I'm on the side of Mustapha and Clifton. Once Caroline has been declared insane or legally incompetent or whatever, I shall have enough money to be free – instead of being ordered about like a dog. Can't you imagine what it's like living with a complete alcoholic? Time after time I have had to fetch Toni to help me get Betty to bed. But before she gets completely drunk, I will have had to listen to her drooling on and on about Caroline's ingratitude to

her. And if she's not blabbering about Caroline, she'll be screaming in rage over some bill I've asked her to pay to the tradesmen.
Betty believes they're all in league to rob her. . . . But Toni leads
a very different life. He's got his own car, and he can go out
whenever he pleases. Betty won't hear a word of criticism against
Toni. She's besotted with him. I have to listen to accounts of his
sexual prowess. . . . And so long as he satisfies her, he can do no
wrong. Toni can leave the house at any moment he likes, yet
Betty only allows me out one evening in the week'.

Sheila's face was now distorted with rage, and her hands were
trembling. 'I hate Betty,' she told Simon. 'I loathe and detest
her.'

'And of course there is yet another reason for you to side with
Mustapha and Clifton,' Simon said quietly. 'You are in love with
Mustapha. You lived with him in Tangier, and now that you're
installed in this villa you have a secret meeting at his house once
a week.'

'So he told you?' Sheila said. 'And it's true. We've been lovers
since we met in Tangier. To see us together in company you'd
never guess it. But we're still very much in love.'

For a moment Simon wondered if he should disillusion her.
But if he tried to, he was certain from her attitude that Sheila
would not believe a word he said.

'My love affair with Mustapha is the only thing that makes life
at all tolerable for me,' Sheila told him.

'You love him so much that you're prepared to obey his
orders?' Simon said.

'Certainly,' Sheila answered.

'And you're prepared to put a drug in the orange juice you
make?' Simon asked.

Simon was watching Sheila closely, and he was almost certain
that he had seen in her face a look of surprise. But Sheila recovered quickly, and she was now staring at him without expression.

'What are you talking about?' She asked. 'Who said anything
about a drug? I may dislike Betty, but I wouldn't want to drug
her.'

'I'm not referring to Betty. I was referring to Caroline.'

'Caroline will be declared insane without any drugs,' Sheila stated. 'I don't know where you got such a stupid idea.'

'I thought that was part of your instructions,' Simon told her.

'Certainly not,' Sheila answered. 'But in any case, you must remember that you've been told not to interfere in any way with what I do.'

Sheila looked at the watch she was wearing. 'It's late,' she said. 'I must go and get dressed in case Betty calls for me. I'll see you later.' Sheila nodded, as if in agreement with what she herself had said. Then she turned away from him and moved towards the door.

Simon waited until he could no longer hear her footsteps. Then he made his way across to Caroline's apartment.

Chapter 18

The door was locked. Simon knocked.

'Who is it?' Caroline asked in a sleepy voice.

'Paul,' he replied.

Caroline unlocked the door and opened it. She was wearing a white bathrobe. He kissed her, but she did not respond.

'I thought you were sleeping with me last night,' Caroline said.

'I couldn't,' Simon replied.

He took her arm and guided her out of the room and on to the balcony, then he shut the doors. They sat down. 'I had to see Mustapha and Clifton again last night,' Simon said.

'Why?' Caroline extended her legs on a reclining chair. She stared at Simon suspiciously.

'I've found out who is spying on us here. It's Sheila. She's in with Clifton and Mustapha and they want to prove to the specialists that you're insane, and legally incompetent, so that Clifton inherits the fortune.'

Caroline sighed, she looked away across into the garden. 'So it is they who have tried to make me go mad.'

'Yes.'

'But why did you have to see them?' she asked angrily.

Simon took a deep breath. He had tried to persuade himself that the reason he had not told Caroline about his identity had been that he was afraid of losing her confidence or distressing her, but he now realized that at least part of the cause of his secrecy was his fear of turning her against him. He now told Caroline of his own part in the whole affair. When he had finished she looked at him for a time in silence.

'Somehow, I never thought of you as a psychiatrist,' she told him. 'So the shock is not as alarming as you might think. I admit it is a shock all the same.' She turned away from him. Simon felt she was making a great effort to control herself. 'There are two questions I must ask you,' Caroline said very quietly. 'What about the tablets you gave me that first day?'

'The tablets are mild sedatives which I was given in hospital when my head was bad,' Simon explained. 'I assure you they are perfectly harmless. You can forget about them . . . . What is your second question?'

Caroline was silent. Her face looked strained.

'Tell me your second question,' Simon asked quietly.

Caroline spoke in a whisper. 'Was it all a pretence? All of it?' she asked. 'I mean, when you made love to me – was that part of the fake too? I hope not, because there's something I must tell you. When you didn't come and see me last night I was desperately upset, and I couldn't understand why,' she continued. 'Then I realized the truth. At first I thought it must be one of my fantasies. I lay awake for hours thinking about it. But the more I thought, the more I realized the reason I was so terribly upset that you hadn't come. I was upset because I was in love with you. I still am.'

Simon put his arms around her and kissed her on the forehead. As he touched her, he knew for certain that he loved her too. 'You know I'm a crook,' he said. 'You know I can be put in prison tomorrow. But you can be certain that I am in love with you. If it hadn't been for you I would have escaped from this villa – or I would have tried to – long before now.'

'What am I to do?' Caroline asked.

'Today and tomorrow don't eat anything that hasn't come from a sealed tin you have opened yourself. I'm certain they're going to try and dope you. Sheila will put some drug in your orange juice. Pour the juice down the sink, but leave a lipstick mark on the glass so it looks as if you have drunk it. The same goes for your coffee. That will keep Sheila from bothering us. I'd like to stay with you all day. But I can't because it would make Sheila suspicious and she would telephone Mustapha. I'll come up and see you at the hours that Dr Orville would. But when all of them have gone to bed this evening after dinner I'll come up and spend the night here if I may.'

'I'd feel far safer if you did.'

'So that's settled, and I'm very glad.'

Caroline was gazing at him. 'Do you really think the specialists will think I'm all right?' she asked.

'I'm certain they will.'

'And your job as Dr Orville will have finished?'

'Yes.'

'So what will you do?' Caroline asked.

'I'll tell you a great secret,' Simon answered. 'Before I came to this villa I booked a passage to Vera Cruz, the eastern port of Mexico.'

'When does the ship sail?'

'In a fortnight's time,' Simon replied.

'If they say I'm okay,' Caroline said. 'I'll be well off. I'll be 21 and free to do what I like. A journey to Vera Cruz and travels around Mexico sound fascinating. One might even buy a villa there. Would you take me?'

'Are you serious?' Simon asked.

'I swear it,' Caroline replied. 'I want to go to Mexico with you. I want to live with you. But I know it's extremely rash. After all, I don't even know your real name.'

'Simon. Simon Perry,' he told her. 'And I love you very much. Of course I'll take you to Mexico. In fact, I'll take you to any place you like.'

'Simon,' Caroline whispered to herself. 'Simon.'

He kissed her once again on the forehead. 'I must go,' he said. 'Remember I can come back at six for a while without arousing any suspicion.' He moved towards the doors and opened them. 'And remember that I love you,' he said softly.

As he walked back along the corridor he saw the Fatima who was carrying a tray with coffee and a croissant and a glass of orange juice. She smiled at him. '*Sbaa el khair*,' she said. '*Bonjour*'.

'*Bonjour*,' Simon replied as he passed by her.

He met no one else on the way to his room. He took off his

clothes and put on a dressing-gown. Though the sun was shining it was very cold in the room. But the water was hot; he turned on the hot water tap of the bath and shaved himself while it was running. As he was dressing, there was a knock at the door. Azziz came in with a large breakfast tray. A quarter of an hour later there was another knock on the door.

'Come in,' he called out.

The door was opened and Sheila appeared. 'I'm here on one of my secretarial duties,' she announced. 'Betty wants to see you in her bedroom. She's put on fresh make-up in your honour so you'd better keep your distance. See you later.'

Simon put on a jacket, brushed his hair and left his room. Azziz, who was waiting outside his door, nodded to him and led the way along the corridor. He stopped in front of an ornate wooden door. 'Here,' he said with a little bow and left. Simon knocked.

'Come in,' Betty cried out in a hoarse voice. He opened the door and shut it behind him. He was in a large room with baroque white and gilt furniture; there were mirrors set into all the walls. But the room was dominated by a very large baroque bed which was adorned with gilt cherubs. Betty lay propped up against the pillows. In the morning light that came in through the windows her make-up looked very obvious. She was wearing a pink silk negligée embroidered with gold.

'Good morning,' she said to him. 'I'm told you needed a long session with Caroline yesterday?'

'I did,' Simon replied. 'I wanted to make sure that my tablets were working.'

'And were they?' Betty asked.

'Yes,' he replied.

'There's nothing worrying her?' Betty asked.

'Nothing that I could detect.'

'I sent for you because I wanted to make sure that there's nothing disturbing her because, as we both know, tomorrow is the crucial day. Does she dread the examination?'

'No,' Simon replied. 'I think she is now convinced that nothing is wrong with her, so she doesn't have anything to worry about. I'll be visiting her later in the day to make sure that all is well. But I don't think that Caroline should have any visitors today since the doctors are coming tomorrow. I don't want anyone else to see her – not even you or Toni.'

'That's quite reasonable,' Betty answered. 'What about Azziz or the Fatima who brings up her food?'

'I'd rather no-one went into her room. Caroline has plenty of food in the fridge, and she's an excellent cook.'

'One more thing,' Betty said. 'I want you to be in the living room when the doctors arrive at half-past ten tomorrow morning. You won't be allowed to be present when they examine Caroline. None of us will. But I'll explain your presence in the house by saying you're an old friend of the family and have come out to Morocco for a holiday. Do you object?'

'Not at all,' Simon assured her.

She raised her plump arm in dismissal. 'See you later,' Betty said.

Simon found Toni in the living room reading a Moroccan newspaper. 'I wish I could spend more time with you,' Toni told him. 'Let me know if you want an evening in Casablanca. I know all the bars where the prettiest girls are to be found.'

'But after the examination tomorrow,' Simon answered, 'my job will have been done, and I shall be leaving.'

'Not immediately, I hope,' Toni said. 'I know that Betty wants you to stay on for at least a week in case Caroline has a relapse, and I would also like you to stay. As it is, I've got nothing to complain about. Betty is very kind to me. Her kindness is wonderful. But it is nice to have another man to talk to. How did you find Caroline's health this morning?'

'She's very calm,' Simon answered. 'And she is fully prepared for the examination tomorrow.'

'What about Betty?' Toni asked.

'Betty seemed fine.'

'I'm glad. I'm afraid she's been very worried about the doctors' examination. I've been concerned. I know that Betty can be difficult at times – especially when she's had too much to drink. But when you really get to know her, you'll find that she's generous and affectionate. I don't know what I would have done without her help. I'm very fond of her, and I'm sure that when you really get to know her you'll be fond of her too.'

'I expect you're right,' Simon said. 'My trouble at the moment is that I didn't sleep at all well last night. I've eaten a huge breakfast which Azziz brought me. Unless you think it would annoy Betty, I'd like to skip lunch and go up to my room and rest for a while. I've arranged with Caroline that I'll go up and see her at six for a short time. But I told Betty that I don't think Caroline ought to have any visitors today. I want her to rest. Will you make my apologies to Betty and explain that I've gone to have a long siesta?'

'Sure I will, I know Betty won't mind,' Toni answered. 'We'll see you later this evening.'

Chapter 19

At dinner that evening, as usual when there were only four of them, Betty put Simon on her right and Toni on her left. Sheila sat facing her across the table. Betty carried on with a monologue for which Simon was grateful because he was worried and he needed time to think. His meeting with Caroline at 6 o'clock had not been a success; he had arrived to find her over-excited by the prospect of Mexico but anxious about the immediate future. She had followed his instructions regarding food and drink, but she was now convinced that Clifton would devise some plan to derange her mind during the night.

'Promise you'll come back after dinner,' she had kept on saying. 'Promise me.'

Simon had held her in his arms and comforted her as one might a child. 'Yes, I do promise you,' he had said.

Caroline had taken hold of his hand. 'And promise me that we will go together to Mexico,' she added.

Simon had stroked her hair. 'Yes, I do promise. I promise,' he had repeated.

But now, as he listened to Betty telling the story of a production which she had helped to finance at the Haymarket Theatre in London, he tried to assuage the anxiety and the doubt that beset him. He was sure that Clifton and Mustapha would make no further attempt that night because they must believe that Sheila was going to mix the drug in Caroline's coffee or orange juice – or had done so already. He was almost certain that the doctors would find Caroline calm and therefore legally competent. Besides, there was little wrong with Caroline, except for the tensions that Betty caused in her. Why then, he asked himself, was he so disturbed? The reason was clear. He had promised

Caroline that they would travel to Mexico together. He was very much in love with her, but his worries sprang from the fact that he knew she tended to be highly-strung and nervous, and he was afraid that however gently he treated her he might in some way upset her.

At last the evening ended. Simon waited till Betty, Toni and Sheila had gone to their rooms. Then he went over to Caroline's apartment.

Caroline must have been waiting for the sound of his footsteps because she opened the door immediately he reached the threshold. Her eyes were bright. 'I've been thinking about you ever since you left,' Caroline said. 'I'm certain that our decision to leave this country and go to Mexico together is the right one. Do you still think so?'

Simon took her hand and kissed it. 'I do, more than ever,' he answered.

'Now that you've arrived,' Caroline said, 'I'm not frightened by what may happen tonight, because you'll be here to guard me. You will stay the whole night, won't you?'

'Yes, of course I will.'

After they had made love, they lay in bed, still holding each other closely.

'Are you nervous at the prospect?'

'What prospect?' Simon asked cautiously.

'The examination tomorrow.'

'Why should I be nervous?' Simon replied. 'I'm sure nothing is wrong with you. I had a long discussion with Dr Orville about you. And he thought the best thing for you would be to leave home and Betty. Besides, I'm sure the two doctors will be honest . . . and Betty has decided to pass me off as an ordinary doctor from London who is a friend of the family, so I don't suppose I'll even be consulted. But what about you? I hope you are not nervous.'

'I shan't be nervous,' Caroline answered, 'so long as you promise to take me to Mexico.'

'I do promise,' Simon told her.

'Whatever happens?' Caroline asked.

149

'Yes,' Simon answered, 'whatever happens.' Gently he moved away from her and got out of the bed. 'But now I'm going to lie on the sofa,' he said, 'because you must get some sleep. Remember I'm in the room next door. And I can assure you that nothing will harm or disturb you tonight.'

Early in the morning, he went into Caroline's room and embraced her while she was still lying half asleep in bed. Then he wished her many happy returns of the day since it was her birthday. He told her to stay in her own rooms, because he considered it was far better for Caroline to be examined in her own apartment.

Simon managed to get back to his room without being seen. He shaved and had a bath. While he was dressing Azziz came in with his breakfast.

'*Shukran,*' Simon said, using one of the few words he had learned in Arabic. 'Thank you.'

Azziz smiled. '*Belajemil,*' he answered. Simon decided this must mean 'don't mention it,' so he smiled back.

When he reached the living-room downstairs he was surprised to find that Betty, Toni and Sheila were already there. Toni was pouring a vodka and tonic for Betty who was ensconced in her usual place on the sofa. Sheila was sitting on a gilt chair though there were several comfortable armchairs to use if she had cared for one. Simon looked at her carefully, trying to discover from the expression on her face whether she could have mixed a drug with Caroline's orange juice. But she seemed both quiet and calm.

'Are you sure that Caroline doesn't mind being left alone this very morning?' Betty asked Simon.

'It's the best thing that could happen,' he answered. 'But it sounds as if she won't be alone for long.'

They could hear a car approaching the main gate.

'I'll go and answer the door,' Toni said. 'Azziz always glares at strangers, and with his turban and tunic, he looks rather alarming to foreigners.'

They waited in silence. Presently Toni returned with the two doctors and introduced them. Both of them were middle-aged. The taller one was called Prescot. His thick grey hair was so carefully arranged that it might have been a wig. He seemed to be the stronger of the two. He moved very carefully as if afraid that any rash movement would disturb his air of authority. The other doctor, called Clark, was a small stout man with large dark eyes and a fleshy nose; he was almost completely bald. His spectacles had thick lenses in a steel-rimmed frame. He appeared to have more vitality than Dr Prescot. Simon thought he resembled a chemist rather than a doctor. When Toni introduced the two of them to Betty, Dr Prescot gave her a little bow. Dr Clark advanced, with what was obviously intended to be a reassuring smile. As planned, Simon was introduced as Dr Orville, a family friend.

After he had introduced them all round Toni left the room.

'I'm sure you will appreciate the difficulty of our position,' Dr Prescot said. 'We cannot take any sides in the matter. Here are our credentials,' he added, handing Betty a long white envelope which was unsealed.

Betty took out the letter it contained and examined it carefully. 'That seems entirely in order,' she said after a pause.

'Our business is perfectly clear, and our report will also be perfectly clear,' Dr Clark told her.

'Unless you have any objection,' Dr Prescot said, patting his head as if to make sure his hair was still there, 'we would prefer to conduct our examination of Miss Caroline Morrison alone with her.' Prescot turned to Simon. 'I'm sure Dr Orville would approve of that,' he said.

'Certainly,' Simon replied.

He then recalled that it was Dr Prescot who Caroline had said was an old friend of her father's, yet he and Betty treated each other as strangers. Simon felt unease, and watched them closely, but their manner was impeccably formal.

'Can I offer you a coffee or a drink?' Betty asked.

'Nothing, thank you,' Dr Prescot replied.

'Perhaps later,' Dr Clark murmured and gave them his reassuring smile.

Betty moved towards the door. 'Then I'll show you both the way,' she said.

Simon and Sheila were left alone.

'Did you manage to spike the orange juice?' Simon asked Sheila with a smile.

'I don't know what you are talking about,' Sheila answered.

Simon noticed that her hands were trembling. 'Is everything going according to plan?' he enquired.

'Yes,' Sheila answered.

'Am I never to be allowed to know what the plan is?' Simon asked.

'I expect not,' Sheila replied. 'I've been ordered not to tell you anything for the time being.'

There was silence as Betty came back into the room.

'Caroline is looking fabulously pretty in her white jacket and trousers,' Betty announced. 'Also, I may add, she seems very relaxed.'

Simon was watching Sheila – he was almost certain that for a moment she looked concerned. Then her lips stretched into a smile. 'That's splendid news,' Sheila said, and she looked quite placid. Simon wondered if she had seen the lipstick on the glass of orange juice.

As she spoke, Toni came back into the room. 'What news of Caroline?' he asked Betty.

'I saw her for an instant,' Betty replied, 'and she looked splendid.'

'Thank heavens for that,' Toni said. 'You know, those two doctors must be getting large fees and expenses. They've hired an enormous new Cadillac to drive them here, and their hotel has packed them a large picnic meal complete with wine.'

'Thank you, Toni,' Betty said. 'You never seem to miss an opportunity for gaining information. And now be an angel and fix me a large vodka and tonic. But don't put in as much tonic as you did last time.'

Toni grinned at her and walked over to the cabinet. 'What about drinks all round?' he asked.

Sheila and Simon both nodded in agreement.

'Drink is one of the ways of making time pass by,' Sheila announced suddenly.

'Of all the platitudes which you utter,' Betty told her, 'that one at least has a grain of truth in it.'

Although they tried to lighten the atmosphere, all four of them were aware of an impending crisis. Betty began once again on her repertoire of the famous people she had known in London. She told them what Ivor had said to Binkie and what Emlyn had said to Edith. Simon found that the long wait for the decision was anguish. He began to wonder if his certainty that there was nothing wrong with Caroline could be correct. After all, it was based only on his own common-sense. And why did Sheila appear so calm? Probably because she had indeed observed the mark of the pale lipstick on the glass when Azziz brought the tray down to the kitchen.

Toni had evidently decided that Sheila's dictum that drink made the time pass by was correct: he would re-fill their glasses whenever he had a chance. For Simon, the time passed as slowly as it had when he had been buried in the earthquake. He could not forget that he had promised to take Caroline with him 'whatever happened.'

At last they heard footsteps in the patio. Toni moved to open the door. Dr Prescot and Dr Clark came into the room. The expression on their faces was solemn. But Prescot's grey hair was so settled that presumably nothing could have disturbed him very much. There was a pause. No one spoke. But Prescot did not keep them in suspense any longer. 'Mrs Morrison,' Dr Prescot said, 'our decision is final and absolute. Having made a thorough, detailed examination, we find that your daughter, Caroline Morrison, is completely sane and therefore legally competent to manage her estate.'

For a moment there was silence. Then Betty gave a sob of relief and tried to smile. Suddenly Sheila rose from her chair and left the room.

'In our report,' Dr Clark stated, in a stern professional voice, 'we are bound to make various observations on Caroline's state of mental and physical health. But that does not affect our decision, which will be absolutely final so far as the trustees of the Morrison estate are concerned.'

Toni immediately got up. There was a look of joy on his face. 'Let's drink to it,' he suggested.

'After all, now that you have made your decision you can share a glass of wine with us,' Betty said to them.

Dr Clark's face looked less serious. Toni crossed the room quickly and opened one of the doors of the cabinet. On its red lacquered shelf was a magnum of champagne. The glasses stood beside it.

'You seem to have been optimistic,' Dr Clark remarked.

Toni opened the bottle and began to fill the glasses. 'That's because what I've seen of Caroline has convinced me personally that there's never been anything wrong with her,' Toni replied.

'Of course she's completely all right,' Betty said. 'She always has been.'

'But we are all grateful for your confirmation,' Toni said, as he handed round the glasses. 'Let's drink to it,' he repeated.

They raised their glasses and drank.

'Where has Sheila gone?' Betty demanded.

'I can't imagine,' Toni replied. 'But we can easily get on without her.'

'When are you returning to New York?' Betty asked, turning to Dr Prescot who was standing beside her.

'This evening, on the night flight from Casablanca,' Dr Prescot answered.

'You see, we too were optimistic,' Dr Clark said. 'But as a new friend rather than as a doctor, may I offer a word of advice? I gather from Caroline that she lives an almost hermit-type of life. I consider this most unhealthy. I think Caroline should be persuaded to go out and mix with people of her own age. Complete seclusion is doing her no good.'

'Thank you, Dr Clark,' Betty replied with a smirk of satisfaction that she had remembered his name correctly.

Toni was going round the room filling up their glasses when they heard the front door bell ring.

'I wonder who that could be?' Betty asked.

Simon's instinct told him it was trouble. It had all been too easy, too smooth; now he knew Clifton would come to take his revenge.

Chapter 20

They heard the deep voice of Azziz speaking in Arabic. He was answered in Arabic. Then the door was opened, and Sheila showed Mustapha and Dr Orville into the living-room. Dr Orville was on crutches. He was wearing his old jacket and flannel trousers, his head had been freshly bandaged. Mustapha was dressed in his cashmere turtle-neck sweater and tight-fitting trousers from which his snakeskin shoes protruded. Clifton followed them. He was wearing the same stained T-shirt and jeans. The worry-beads now hung round his neck; he was barefooted. He was poised unsteadily on his feet, and as he moved lethargically it was obvious that he was drugged. In contrast his expression was frantic, he looked astonished and desperate.

Betty glared at Sheila. 'How dare you invite these people to my villa?' she demanded.

Sheila was silent.

'Well, Clifton, I can see you haven't improved over the years,' Betty said. 'What do you mean by coming here?'

'I thought I might be able to help,' he answered in a strained voice.

'And who are these people you've brought with you?' Betty enquired. She was shaking with anger.

'This is a close friend of mine called Mustapha who I brought along as a witness,' Clifton said. 'But the gentleman on crutches is the most important person I want you to meet. Betty, may I introduce Dr Orville to you?'

'What are you talking about?' Betty asked. She pointed to Simon. 'He is Dr Orville. He's an old friend who is staying with us.'

Clifton moved unsteadily towards her.

'You're wrong,' he said. 'And at least you know that he's not an old friend. You met him less than a week ago.'

'What lies!' Betty cried.

'The man who has been staying in your villa is an imposter and a crook,' Clifton said. 'He is not Dr Orville. His name, in fact, is Simon Perry. What is more, he has probably been administering very powerful sedatives to Caroline.'

Both Prescot and Clark were watching the scene in silent disapproval.

'Absolute nonsense!' Betty exclaimed.

'Dr Orville, Mustapha and I suspected something like this would happen,' Clifton said.

'We were in the café at the bottom of the hill waiting for the result,' Mustapha explained. 'As soon as Sheila telephoned me we thought we must come to expose this fraud. Your daughter has been drugged to appear sane.'

'Whatever the name of your house-guest may be,' Dr Prescot said to Betty, 'we can assure you that Caroline is not under any sedation. Dr Clark took samples and she was completely free of any drugs or toxic substances.'

Simon was silent. He now understood why Sheila had left the room so suddenly. She must have realized that either the drug she was using had had no effect or that Caroline had been warned not to drink her orange juice. Sheila had immediately gone to telephone the café where they were waiting.

'In cases of this kind,' Dr Clark said, 'symptoms of sedation are the first thing we always look for and our tests are conclusive. We can assure you that Caroline has not been drugged.'

'Isn't it possible that the drug was undetectable?' Clifton asked.

'Impossible,' Dr Prescot replied. 'If she had been under sedation of any kind, our examination would have shown it.'

'Doesn't it concern you that Caroline has been looked after by a man who is both an imposter and a crook?' Sheila asked.

Dr Orville moved slowly forward on his crutches. 'Perhaps I can help you,' he said. 'Until today I have been kept a prisoner by the two men who brought me here. One is a vicious sadist, and the other is certainly a hopeless dope addict. I have only been brought to this villa in order to expose Simon Perry. I am Dr Orville.'

'You're not Dr Orville,' Betty said to him. '*You* are the impostor,' she turned to Simon. 'Tell them who you are,' she ordered.

'May I make a suggestion?' Simon asked. 'May I suggest that this matter does not affect the judgement of our two eminent specialists?' He was amazed at how calm he felt, how fulfilled he was that the truth would be known.

Dr Prescot turned to Betty. His expression was once again stern. 'I agree with that suggestion,' he said coldly. 'Neither Dr Clark nor I need to be embroiled in what would seem to be a private family affair. Our judgement remains unchanged, and I think we should leave you now. We must thank you for your hospitality.'

Dr Clark finished his glass of champagne. His reassuring smile was becoming strained. 'May I join my colleague in thanking you for your hospitality, Mrs Morrison?' he asked. 'You will be hearing from the trustees very shortly. Goodbye to you all.' He gave them a little nod and turned to go. His smile vanished as he moved.

Toni opened the door for the two doctors. Azziz was standing in the patio. Toni spoke to him in Arabic. He bowed.

'Azziz will show you to your car,' Simon heard Toni say. 'I must apologize for the unwelcome intrusion. Goodbye to you both.'

As Toni came back into the room Betty turned to Simon. 'Tell them who you are,' she repeated.

Dr Orville spoke to Simon. 'You've got to help me,' he told him.

'Tell them who you are,' Betty demanded yet again; she was now glaring at Simon.

'I'm sorry to disillusion you,' Simon answered quietly. 'I am afraid it will come as a shock. But, in fact, I am not Dr Orville. As you've been told, my name is Simon Perry. . . . The real Dr Orville is the man on crutches.'

Simon put his hand in the breast pocket of his jacket and took out a folder of travellers' cheques, some money, and an important looking document. He handed them to Dr Orville. 'These belong to you,' Simon said to him. 'Don't worry. I'll look after you somehow.'

He was an honest man again. No longer a crook. He was himself again.

'Will you rescue me from these two liars and scoundrels?'

'Yes,' Simon replied. 'I will.'

'Thank you, Simon Perry,' Dr Orville said. 'I do trust you now.'

Clifton moved unsteadily towards Dr Orville. 'You idiot!' he cried. 'You've wrecked everything.' Clifton raised a trembling hand to hit Dr Orville, but Simon quickly grabbed hold of his arm. Mustapha moved towards him holding a knife. Toni sprang forward and clasped Mustapha's arm and twisted his wrist savagely. The knife dropped onto the floor. Toni kicked it away.

'I always knew you were a bad lot,' Betty said to Clifton. 'Now get out or be thrown out.' She glanced towards Toni, who nodded.

Mustapha turned to Simon. 'Are you prepared for me to go to the police and expose you as a criminal fraud?'

'I wouldn't call in the police if I were you,' Toni told him. 'They know quite a bit about you already. So now get out, and stay away from this villa. You've lost the game, and there's nothing you can do now.'

'Lost the game!' Clifton screamed and turning towards Betty, he continued. 'You must have bribed those two specialists. You know my half-sister is a lunatic. What about all those fantasies she had about me, and before that, with whatshisname . . . that negro, seeing you and him together? She's been lying on psychiatrists' couches for years, spilling out all the sexual filth she could dream up about you and about me.' He thumped his chest, and glared at Betty. 'Can you deny it?'

'Of course I deny it,' Betty shouted. 'All this rubbish you've just cooked up yourself. You're drugged and senseless. Now get out of my house. All of you.' Imperiously, she pointed to the door.

Clifton turned away.

At the instant that Mustapha prepared to leave, Sheila rushed up to him. 'When shall we meet?' she asked.

'Meet!' Mustapha exclaimed. 'After what's happened? When you have completely failed us? Do you think I want to meet you? You really think I want to meet *you*? You stupid bitch! What vanity you must have to imagine that your looks attracted me! I hope I will never see you again so long as I live.'

Mustapha turned his back on her and followed Clifton out of the door.

As he spoke, Sheila had begun to cry. The tears made the black mascara on her eye-lashes run down her cheeks. She looked around as if in the hope that someone could help her, but no-one spoke. Then, still weeping, she left the room.

'There's another traitor for you!' Betty cried. She was now close to hysteria. She pointed a trembling hand at Simon, then turned to Dr Orville. 'If you knew that this man was an impostor why did you let him stay here?'

'I've already tried to explain, Mrs Morrison,' Dr Orville said. 'I was a prisoner.'

Betty's hand was now shaking as she pointed her finger at Simon. 'Do you intend to let this man get away with his fraud?' she asked Dr Orville.

'Yes,' Dr Orville replied.

'Well, I *don't* intend him to get away with it,' Betty announced. 'I shall call the police immediately.'

Toni spoke very gently to her. 'I don't think I should do that,' Toni said. 'As you know, when we first met I was not on the best of terms with the police. And in Morocco the police have long memories.'

'Then do you advise me to let him go?' Betty asked.

'I think it might be wiser,' Toni replied.

'I've got very little to say in my defence,' Simon said. 'When we became friends, I did all I could to help Caroline. For instance I discovered that the Moroccan girl on the balcony wasn't a hallucination and I was able to convince Caroline of the fact. What's more, I had reason to believe that today or yesterday

160

Sheila would be instructed by Mustapha, who had a great influence on her, to put a hallucinatory drug in her orange juice or coffee. And I persuaded Caroline not to drink or eat anything that she hadn't prepared herself.'

'You were still ready to accept the money I would have given Dr Orville as the second part of his fee,' Betty told him.

'I'm not sure about that,' Simon answered. 'But I think I probably would have taken the money. However, as it is, I think you should pay the money to Dr Orville.'

'I didn't do the job,' Dr Orville said. 'I won't take the money, but I'm grateful to you for the suggestion.' As he spoke, he moved towards the nearest armchair and sat down.

The door opened and Caroline appeared. She looked radiant. 'What are you all doing standing around here in a state of gloom?' Caroline asked. 'Don't you see, mother, that we've won? I'm rich, and you'll now by no means be poor.'

Betty crossed the room and kissed Caroline. 'I know my darling,' she said. 'It's a wonderful relief to us. I never doubted you were really competent to manage your fortune, but I was afraid that the doctors might for some reason be biased.'

'They were a bit frightening at first,' Caroline said, 'but after a while they relaxed, and I found them both charming.'

'Caroline, I'm afraid there is something I must warn you about,' Betty stated. 'I must tell you that we have proof that your dear friend, who calls himself Dr Orville, is an imposter. The real Dr Orville is the man with crutches sitting in the armchair. Your friend is a complete crook and a scheming charlatan.'

'He did something crooked,' Caroline said, 'which is another matter.'

'You don't seem very surprised,' Betty remarked.

'I'm not,' Caroline answered. 'Because I knew already.'

'You knew?' Betty exclaimed. 'When did you know?'

'Simon told me yesterday morning,' Caroline replied. 'In fact, he told me all about himself.'

'You knew?' Betty repeated. 'Yet you didn't tell me?'

'I thought it better to let things ride until after the examination,' Caroline answered.

161

'You've shown a complete lack of trust in me,' Betty complained, her voice quivering bitterly. 'You're quite heartless. You should have confided in me.'

'Don't blame Caroline,' Simon said. 'It's all my fault. Caroline took the news of my true identity quite calmly, and I didn't want any scenes before the examination.'

'So *you* didn't trust me either,' Betty said. Her protuberant eyes were misty with tears.

'Once he had taken on my identity,' Dr Orville explained, 'Simon Perry must have found it difficult to trust anyone.'

'Do you take his side?' Betty asked Dr Orville. 'After all the wrong he's done you?'

'I don't take any side,' Dr Orville told her. 'But you must admit that Simon Perry may have been largely responsible for getting your daughter through the examination, for somehow he managed to prevent your secretary from drugging her – and that was part of their plan.'

'I shall dismiss Sheila today,' Betty declared. 'But Caroline didn't need Simon Perry's help. She was always suspicious of Sheila.'

Toni moved across the room and put an arm round Betty's shoulder. 'Betty, now don't be angry,' he told her quietly. 'I'm sure that Dr Orville is right, and if he can forgive Simon, I'm certain that you can.'

Betty was near to crying. 'At least you trust me, Toni,' she said.

Toni kissed her gently on the forehead. 'You know I trust you, Betty,' he murmured. 'And now, if you'll let me, and if Dr Orville approves, I could drive him to the Casablanca airport and put him on the next plane to Geneva. I can get him fixed up with a passport in town.'

'Certainly,' Betty said. Her voice was calmer now.

'Thank you,' Dr Orville said to Betty and Toni. 'This has all been a terrifying and horrible experience for me, and I need rest and quiet, a long convalescence.' He paused. 'But what about Simon Perry? I'm worried about him. Of course, Clifton can't go to the police because his only valid witness to prove that Simon was guilty of impersonation is myself, and I shan't be in Morocco. I'm worried that Clifton may think up some other way of harming him.'

Caroline went over to Simon and took his arm. She stared round the room defiantly. 'From now onwards I hope that Simon will be my responsibility,' Caroline told them. 'I intend to leave Morocco as soon as I can. If Simon is willing I'll take him along with me.'

'I'm very willing,' Simon said, smiling at her.

Caroline smiled back at Simon. 'You never know,' she said, 'but there may be times when even a fake psychiatrist can be useful.'

'When did you make this stupid decision?' Betty asked her.

'During the last two days,' Caroline answered steadily. 'And the decision isn't stupid to me.'

'Nor to me,' Dr Orville said suddenly. 'When I was shut up in Mustapha's house and Simon Perry was brought there by force I had a long conversation with him. Let me tell you as a doctor I'm certain that at heart he's not a crook. Also, from what I have heard about Caroline I'm convinced it would be a good thing for her to leave her present environment and go out and see the world.'

'Thank you for your confidence in me,' Simon said to him.

Dr Orville nodded to Simon. He got up and walked on his crutches towards Betty. 'I feel sure that Caroline's decision is right,' Dr Orville said. 'Please don't worry. And allow me to thank you for letting me be driven to the airport.' He stretched out his right arm and took her hand. 'Goodbye, Mrs Morrison,' he said. He turned towards Caroline. 'And congratulations on your birthday,' he added, smiling at her. Once again he nodded to Simon. 'Goodbye Simon Perry,' he said. 'Stick to your own name, and stick to your decision.'

Toni opened the door for him, and together they left the room.

'For all you may say,' Betty stated, looking at Caroline, 'I still think you're being very rash. The fact remains that you hardly know this Simon Perry.'

'I'm aware of the risk I'm taking,' Caroline replied. 'But it's a risk for both of us, and I love him.'

Betty took Caroline's hands and stared into her eyes. 'Do you intend to leave me all alone?' she asked. Her voice was quavering.

Caroline looked back at her calmly. 'You've got enough money,' she said. 'Don't forget that I promised you a third of the estate. You've got Toni who is devoted to you, and should you ever run into debt you know that I would always help.'

'So I should hope,' Betty said bitterly, turning away from Caroline, 'after the care I've taken of you for all these years.'

'I won't forget,' Caroline answered.

Simon had been silent. He was pleased with the calmness that Caroline was displaying in the conflict with her mother. She seemed to have found a new dignity. But the fact that Caroline was now very rich disturbed him. She was a different person from the highly-strung, rather pathetic girl he had met in her apartment that first day. However, he realized that he was now bound to travel with her to Mexico. At first, this realization alarmed him. Then, with a sudden shock of surprise, he became aware that he was longing for the journey, for he discovered that though she was no longer the nervous, uncertain, hesitant person he had first known, he was still in love with her.

Simon turned to Betty. 'Caroline and I are in love,' he told her.

'It's easy to be in love with a young and extremely rich girl,' Betty answered.

Simon felt a surge of fury, but he made himself remember what Toni had told him about the kind side of Betty's nature. He tried to think of something to say in his own defence. But it was Caroline who spoke. 'I think you should know that Simon and I made our decision to live together before the doctor's verdict,' she said.

'Do you honestly believe that if you had been declared insane he would have kept his promise?' Betty asked.

'Yes, I do,' Caroline replied. 'Most certainly I do. You see, I think I've found someone who really will look after me.' Caroline went up to Betty and gazed at her. Simon was surprised to see the look of affection in her eyes. 'Please believe me, mother,' she said. 'Please give us your blessing.'

Betty hesitated for a moment. It seemed to Simon that she was making a great effort to control herself. Then Betty sighed. 'It looks as if you have made up your mind,' she said to Caroline after a pause. 'I can only hope that the two of you will be happy together.'

Chapter 21

Simon and Caroline were in their cabin drinking a bottle of champagne before dinner, which had been brought by the steward of the French cargo boat, which was now 2 days away from Vera Cruz. The ship was rolling gently on a smooth sea. They could hear the splash of the waves above the throb of the engine.

Caroline sipped her drink and stared at Simon over the rim of the glass, then she put the glass down, stretched out and took his hand. 'Darling,' she said, 'I think it's only just gone.'

Simon frowned. 'What?'

'You've been worrying over something and now it's gone.'

Simon laughed. 'Maybe you're right.'

'What was it? I felt it. A kind of dark shadow within you, ever since we boarded this boat, and today it seemed – all different.'

Simon nodded. 'Yes, I think it is.'

She kissed him. 'Don't keep anything from me.'

He paused for a moment, then said. 'The day before we left I had a talk with Betty. She wanted to see me. It was just that.' Simon shrugged. 'Nothing really.'

'But whatever Betty said worried you? Is that it?' Caroline asked.

Simon filled their glasses. 'I don't want to talk about it.'

'Please, my darling, I don't want anything between us. And if my mother upset you in some kind of way, I have a right to know.' Caroline rose and stretched herself. She was tanned and Simon thought she looked radiant, as if she had been freed from a dark cell.

'She didn't try and make out you were a fortune hunter, I hope?' Caroline asked with a smile.

Simon shook his head.

'You know,' Caroline said. 'When we get to Vera Cruz I want us to be married. Because there's no-one, no-one I love more in the world.' She knelt down beside him, and flung her arms about his neck. She buried her face in his shoulder, then whispered. 'Now tell me, how did Betty upset you?'

He laughed. 'You are a little schemer, using every ploy to extract information from me.'

'Well?' Caroline waited.

'Your mother wanted to warn me. I think, in fact, that it was her last effort to part us. She said she had lied to me, and would have lied to the real Dr Orville as well.'

'In what way?' Caroline whispered, still clinging to him.

Simon put his arms around her and held her tightly. 'Betty wanted you to stay with her. She didn't want you to go away, so she told me more lies.'

'Oh Simon,' Caroline said, 'do tell me what outrageous things she came up with this time.'

'Your mother said you had been diagnosed about 2 years ago as a schizophrenic, and one that suffers from hallucinations. You have never been able to tell the difference between reality and your own fantasy wishes or desires. She said you were incurable.' He held her very tight. He listened to her calm voice answering him.

'What did you say?'

'I told her that because of her own sexual promiscuity she had had to make out you were suffering from these delusions and that she must now stop lying. I told her that you must be free. I told her that we loved each other. And I think I also said that everyone else was mad except for us two.'

'You were marvellous,' Caroline sat back on her haunches and stared up at him with a look of wonder. 'I do adore you.'

'Then let's finish the champagne.'

Caroline rose from the floor and stretched herself again. 'What would you like me to wear this evening?'

She was in a white silk slip that clung to her body and showed her slim thighs and small buttocks. Simon thought she ought to wear that and nothing else, for she looked perfect. 'The white dress,' he said, 'because you're so deliciously brown now and your hair seems to be spun gold. I can't believe my luck. Don't you think I'm the most fortunate creature on earth?'

'We both are,' she said, opening a cupboard and fingering the dresses that hung there.

'Can we put the cork back into the bottle?' Caroline asked.

Simon laughed. 'I'm sure that's one of the questions that some of your real psychiatrists might have asked you.'

Caroline smiled at him. 'It's exactly like one of their questions,' she replied. 'But I mean it literally.'

'Certainly we can put the cork back if we trim it down a little,' Simon answered. 'But what's the point when the bottle's empty?'

'Because I've just had an idea – though I admit it's silly,' Caroline told him. 'I thought we could record how happy we are by putting a message in the bottle. Then we'll throw the bottle overboard, and it will float away on the ocean to some distant shore.'

'I don't think it's all that silly,' Simon said, smiling, as he always did at her whims. 'Why not?' He searched in a drawer of the cupboard beside the bed and brought out a pad of paper and a pen.

'You do the writing,' Simon told her, 'because you write more clearly than I do. But we'll compose the message jointly. Each of us can dictate a separate sentence. You begin.'

Simon took the cork and began to trim it with a penknife. For an instant his mind swung back to the day he had found a knife in the playing-fields at school. But he found the memory no longer had the power to hurt him.

'Shall I start now?' Caroline asked. Simon nodded.

Caroline spoke aloud as she wrote. 'Whoever finds this bottle,' Caroline began, 'and reads this message should know that it comes from two people who are very much in love and have enjoyed the most wonderful voyage on a ship heading for Vera Cruz.'

'There was a time when one of us was supposed to be insane,' Simon dictated, 'and the other was supposed to be a crook, but

168

both suppositions were wrong.'

'They were completely wrong,' Caroline said as she wrote, 'and we are now sailing away to safety – to start a new life together in a place where no one will know us.'

'We want to share our happiness so we are writing this message,' Simon continued.

Caroline rummaged in her bag and took out a $100 bill which she rolled up and put in the bottle. 'We are enclosing $100,' she wrote, 'and we hope that it may provide as much pleasure as we are experiencing.'

Caroline looked up at Simon. 'Do you think we should sign our message?' she asked.

'Let's just put our Christian names,' Simon suggested.

'Caroline and Simon,' Caroline wrote. Then she tore the sheet of paper from the pad, rolled it up, and put it into the bottle. Simon took the cork and screwed it down tightly.

'Let's go out,' Caroline suggested, 'and send our message on its way.'

They went out on deck. The sun was just about to set. A great fiery ball of vivid scarlet and orange hung in a sky which it filled with the dense colours of a prism from yellow to purple. They stood there staring in wonder as the sun gradually descended and then as it neared the horizon it moved quickly, zooming down as if tugged by some great invisible titan.

Half of the sun remained and in that second Caroline said: 'Now.' She kissed the bottle and handed it to Simon, and he kissed it solemnly. Then with an extravagant gesture, he threw it out to sea. The sun vanished from the sky.

In silence they watched the bottle bobbing in the water until it disappeared in the frothy wake of the ship. Caroline turned to Simon. There were tears in her eyes. 'Aren't we a couple of sentimental fools?' she asked.

'That's because we're in love,' Simon replied, as he put his arm round her.

She leaned against him. The sky was changing colour, the crimson turned to indigo, the gold was tinted with vermilion streaks.

'And today you became free of whatever horrid things my mother had told you,' Caroline whispered. 'She tried to poison you against me.'

He kissed her. 'Yes, today I realized that.' He paused. 'I'm ashamed. Can you forgive me?'

Caroline drew away from him. 'Of course,' she said. 'You mustn't be ashamed about it. There was still some residue of doubt about me?'

'I suppose there was,' he answered gloomily. Then he smiled. 'But it's gone and soon we shall be married.'

They turned to go down to dinner. 'And then,' Caroline said, 'I want to halve the estate. I want half of it in your name. I'm not going to be the rich woman dispensing money to her husband. It is too humiliating for you.' She kissed him lightly on the cheek. 'Don't say no or anything. It's sensible. I shall do it without your agreement anyway.'

Simon shrugged. 'Money, for the first time in my life, seems irrelevant.'

'That's because we have so much.' She paused. 'And poor Clifton, I wonder sometimes whether I should not have been fair and given him half of what I have.'

Simon laughed. 'You're much too generous. It's what your father wanted. After all, you were the one he loved.'

Caroline suddenly clung to him. 'Oh Simon, you know I still miss him. How I wish you had known him. He was so gentle, so patient and sweet to me.'

They sat at a table and ate ripe melon as the ship carried them on the smooth sea towards a new continent. But Caroline looked withdrawn as if remembering her father had made her melancholy. She toyed with the grilled tunny fish and salad, then pushed the plate away and lit a cigarette.

'Darling,' she said. 'I'm going to walk on deck. Just for a while. I want to imagine our champagne bottle reaching some sandy beach and giving someone a little of our happiness.'

'Of course,' he said, rising from the chair. 'Don't forget, it might reach some native fisherboy who won't understand a word of it.'

'But he'll get it translated,' she said. 'I'll be back soon. I want some pineapple. You can order it for me.'

Simon turned back to his plate; the fresh tunny was delicious. He ate his and then the piece she had left. He had only told her part of that scene with Betty; he would never tell her all of it. It was now buried and he would soon forget it too. It had been the last, and in some ways the most horrible experience of them all in Morocco. God, how he hated that country. He would never go back there.

Betty had asked him to come to her bedroom that morning. She was wearing a negligée of coffee-coloured lace with abundant frills around the neck and sleeves, her face as usual had been heavily made up. There was a glass of brandy or whisky on the dressing table, among the cosmetics and jewellery.

Betty had stared into the mirror at his reflection, as if she could not endure to tell him face to face. 'It's my duty,' she had said. 'I can't let you go on this voyage with Caroline. She must stay here with me. If you're so much in love, you're welcome to stay too. That's my offer.'

When he had refused she had continued. 'Then go to hell, for that's where Caroline will take you. My God, you're a naive fool. . . .'

'You've got a third of the estate,' Simon had broken in. 'What more do you want? To have control of all your daughter's money?'

At this Betty had turned and stared at him scornfully. 'No. What I want is to continue to care for my daughter. Because I'm the only person she has in the world who understands her. I tricked you and the specialists into their verdict. But they were wrong, as Clifton well knew.'

'What the hell do you mean?' he had said.

Then icily Betty had related to him the diagnosis of the psychiatrists. After they had come to Morocco Betty had flown to Switzerland and taken Caroline with her. It was in Switzerland that Caroline had had extensive treatment. The American doctors knew nothing of this.

Simon had told her that she was a jealous, possessive mother, a compulsive liar, who would go to any lengths to keep her daughter under her control. And now it was not only her daughter but a vast fortune she would have at her disposal as well. His words had infuriated her.

Betty had swept the bottles from the dressing table and turned towards him. She had paced the room, swore and cursed at him. 'Caroline is two people, you fool, can't you understand it? You have only seen the first Caroline, the lovely, serene, innocent girl. No longer innocent, because of you. You've taken advantage of her.' She had spat at him like a fishwife. 'Wait until you see the other person buried inside her – the wild hysterical madwoman, chewing her hair, scratching her face and breasts, thinking she is an eagle that can fly, flapping her arms like this and trying to throw herself off from some great mountain.'

He had stared in horror at Betty as she had aped her words. This ageing painted grotesque, waving her arms with their frilled sleeves and jumping about the room like a circus clown. Simon felt such deep nausea he had wanted to be sick.

'If she was ever ill, it was caused by you,' Simon had shouted. 'That's what Dr Orville thought too. We spoke about Caroline together. That's what he said, you were the cause of the trouble.'

'Me,' Betty had echoed, one hand on her full breasts and stopping in the room, facing Simon and staring at him with such resentful hatred he felt again sick in his stomach. 'I, who have protected my poor child from everything wicked in this world. And what returns have I had from her? Only these filthy lies told about me.' Betty was a good actress, Simon thought. She was now doing her Bernhardt tragedy act. Where's your wooden leg, he had thought meanly.

'I despise you,' he had said. Then he had left the room.

As he had walked away down the corridor he heard the sound of more breaking glass. Simon thought: if anyone needs a psychiatrist it is that foul-minded creature.

This scene had not so much left any doubts, but it had depressed and darkened part of his happiness when the voyage had begun. Simon had been worrying about how he could stop Caroline from ever seeing her mother again. Betty was utterly selfish and egocentric. When Caroline had said that her mother was only interested in sex and money, she had been right. But Betty was consumed by greed; she had to have more sex and more money, a continual flow, and even then Simon knew she would be hungry and unsatisfied.

In the first few days of the voyage Simon had asked casually other questions which worried him. Caroline had spoken about the two specialists.

'They were so earnest and sober. I mean, darling, just one look at them and I should have sunk into a depression. But I knew you were there waiting for me,' she had said.

'That reminds me,' Simon had asked her. 'You remember you told me that Dr Prescot was an old friend of your father's?'

'Mmm, I know I did, but I got the name mixed up. I think that was Pritchard; I got quite a shock when he walked in, because I was expecting someone else.'

'What questions did they ask?' Simon had enquired.

Caroline had laughed. 'Oh Simon, all that old stuff. They went right back into childhood again, over the same ground. Joshua and Betty. Clifton and Betty. I mean, they had my file there, didn't they?' Simon had nodded and then asked what Caroline had said to them. 'I was terribly cool and civilized. I told them that it was all untrue. In my adolescent mess, I said, or something like that, I had imagined Joshua with Betty and then Betty seducing Clifton that long, hot summer.'

'But it was true?' Simon had asked.

Caroline had laughed again. 'Yes, of course it was. But if I stuck to my story it meant, according to that file, that I was still clinging on to my hallucinations.'

'Of course,' Simon agreed.

'So the specialists knew then that I had come through my adolescence and at twenty-one was free of all that junk.' She had paused. 'I think I quite impressed them.'

'I know you did,' Simon had said, squeezing her hand. 'Because when they returned to us they were completely convinced.'

Some days later he had said to Caroline. 'Clifton thought you were insane. He denied that he had ever stayed for any length of time in that Connecticut house.'

'Clifton wanted me insane,' Caroline had whispered to him. They had just made love and she was lying in his arms. The warm air from the porthole caressed their naked bodies. 'Clifton was bound to deny my story, because he had to prove that I was always out of my mind.' Then she had sighed and murmured 'Poor Clifton.'

Yes, Simon thought – as he stared at the plain white table-cloth, as he sat waiting in the dining-room for Caroline to return – she often said 'poor Clifton', as if they had once been close and affectionate and not the bitter enemies they were now. Well, Clif-ton must be buried with that bitch of a mother. In Vera Cruz he and Caroline would start their new life together, far away from everyone that could hurt them.

He looked up to see Caroline smiling down at him. 'I saw a huge white bird, like a seagull, only much bigger. It circled over the ship. Its wings were outstretched and in the dusk it looked more like a ghost of a bird than a real bird.' She sat down and leaned across the table to hold his hands. He shivered. 'I've had quite enough of ghosts,' he said, thinking of Dr Orville, and the way Clifton had manipulated that poor wrecked figure, to try and send him out of his senses too. 'You know, there is no divid-ing line. I've reached the conclusion that nothing, whether real or unreal, true or false, nothing can be divided absolutely.'

'Yes,' she said. 'I know that. It all merges, fuses into one. That's what I thought when I looked up just now at that great white bird. It may not be real, it may be a ghost, but it is still beautiful whatever it is.'

They returned to their cabin and made love, slowly and lan-guorously, abandoning their bodies to complete sensuality. Could anything be as ecstatic as this, Simon wondered, as he lay quietly next to her naked body.

'Simon,' Caroline said, 'be an angel and go and get my packet of cigarettes. They're on the dressing-table.'

Simon did not stir. He had reached a state of tranquillity that was infinitely precious to him, and he feared that any movement might break his peace of mind. He heard Caroline's words, but it was as if she were speaking in some language that he could not understand.

'Simon,' Caroline said. 'You're already half asleep. Did you hear what I asked you?'

'No,' Simon mumbled.

'I asked you to be an angel and get my packet of cigarettes which are on the dressing-table.'

'"Be an angel",' Simon repeated drowsily. 'That is the phrase your mother always uses when she wants Toni to do something for her.'

'Never mind my mother,' Caroline said. 'Be an angel and go and get my cigarettes. And you might bring me my lighter at the same time.'

'But I do mind your mother,' Simon replied. 'I mind her very much when I think that her influence on you still lingers.'

'Will you go and get my cigarettes?' Caroline demanded.

Simon was now fully awake, and he realized that Caroline was speaking in a peremptory tone reminiscent of her mother. 'You're closer to the dressing-table than I am,' Simon pointed out. 'Why not get the cigarettes yourself?'

'Will you get those cigarettes?' Caroline repeated.

'No, I won't,' Simon answered, trying to keep any trace of exasperation from his voice.

'I've told you I want my cigarettes,' Caroline said. 'Do you hear me?'

Suddenly Simon realized that Caroline was angry. Her tone had become hysterical. 'Get me those cigarettes,' Caroline cried out in a voice trembling with fury.

Simon heard again Betty's voice shrieking at him in her violent rage on that day before they had left Morocco. He was horrified. What had happened to the serene and happy woman he had spent the voyage with? This obviously was her mother's influence. She had been brought up by Betty, had seen Betty fall into the same rages and thought it was the only way to achieve what she wanted. These thoughts raced through his mind as he lay there beside her, still feeling stunned by the change in her.

He knew that if he gave in to all her wiles and demands he

might attain a temporary respite, but it would be at Caroline's expense in every sense of the word, for it would encourage the unstable side of her nature. By pampering her in order to have a quiet time, he would, in fact, be committing yet another act of dishonesty. But he had sworn to himself that he would no longer be a fraud. Simon knew what he must now do – though it would mean taking a risk.

Simon raised himself on one arm and looked down in silence at Caroline's petulant expression. The moment had come. Firmly and deliberately he slapped her face. For an instant Caroline stared up at him in complete amazement. A moment later there was a look of bewilderment in her eyes. Then she put an arm around his neck and closed her eyes. And Simon decided there would be peace – at least for a while.

Chapter 22

Later in the night Simon awoke. Immediately he became aware that Caroline was no longer in the bed. 'Caroline,' he called out softly. There was no reply. He got up and crossed the cabin to the bathroom and opened the door. The room was empty. Suddenly he remembered Caroline's fit of hysteria when he had refused to fetch the cigarettes from the dressing table.

Yet he had solved that problem; he had shown who was the master and she had been shocked, but then she had immediately understood and enfolded him in her arms. He must have slept almost immediately. He recalled her sudden trembling and he, though half asleep, soothing her. She had then nestled close to him. That was all he could remember.

'Oh Caroline, you silly creature,' he muttered to himself. Then he flung on a T-shirt and hauled on his cotton trousers. He yawned and stretched himself. 'Bloody mad time to go for a walk on deck.' Then he thought why was he worrying? If Caroline had woken up and couldn't get back to sleep it was the most natural thing for her to take a stroll.

He went out into the alley-way and up the companion-way on to the deck. He could see no-one. He looked into the dimly-lit bridge. There was a seaman at the wheel but no-one else. He began to climb the companion-way that led to the top deck. As he climbed the ladder he could see the head of a seaman who was standing at a ship's wheel, open to the sky and surrounded by a wooden rail. He had been told that this top-bridge was meant for navigating through coral. But he could see that the dark-skinned sailor was not looking out to sea but downwards. As Simon climbed further up the ladder he could see there was something white crouched between his parted legs. The sailor had lowered his trousers. The white shape kneeling between his legs was a woman. She was wearing white pyjamas. It was Caroline.

When he saw what she was doing he knew. . . . He remembered Betty and Joshua, Caroline's negro servant, and the scene in Betty's bedroom which Caroline had witnessed, and had then run to her father and screamed about Betty's cannibalism. Her mother was eating the black servant. Her mother . . . Betty? But Betty had denied the story and Caroline swore it was true and now Caroline . . . oh Christ, no.

Simon stood there, unable to move. Suddenly Caroline's head began to jerk. An instant later she turned and saw him. Her mouth was smeared. For an instant Simon stared at her in disgust. Then he moved away swiftly and went down the steps to their cabin. He poured himself a drink. He had taken three gulps when Caroline came in. Her face was expressionless as she sat down at the dressing table. In silence she took up a handkerchief, looked into the mirror and wiped her lips. Then she took a comb and tried to arrange her disordered hair.

'You bitch,' Simon said. 'And you pretended you were shocked by what your mother did. Get out. Go back to your black sailor.'

Caroline went on staring at herself in the mirror. Then she smiled at her reflection. 'Don't give me orders,' she said in a calm and distant voice. 'Or I shall have you removed.'

'What the hell do you mean?' Simon shouted. 'Removed? I'm the man you're supposed to be in love with.'

'Oh him,' Caroline said. She took the handkerchief and rubbed the mirror with it, as if it was dirty. 'I shouldn't think he'd be back, would you?'

He stepped towards her and took hold of her. 'Who? What? Caroline, what are you talking about?' He began to shake her shoulders. Her head lolled to and fro like a puppet. Her blonde hair fell over her face. She began to laugh.

Simon let go of her. 'I don't understand,' he murmured quietly.

Caroline began to half chant some words. 'My sweet Joshua in the stables every day. Undress me Joshua. Rich little white girl. Take your revenge on the white race, Joshua. You're much too big for me. And you mustn't be found out Joshua. If they find you out they'll lynch you Joshua. Hang you from a tree and cut off your prick, cut it off, your pride, Joshua and feed it to the dogs, Joshua.' She stopped that strange sing-song, then lowered her voice so that it almost became a whine. 'I'm so small Joshua, but you like it, no breasts, no hair, but you like it, caress me Joshua, that's right my black darling, caress and soothe me.' She had closed her eyes, her head thrown back. She swung her body from side to side and then moaned.

Simon watched her. He put his hands over his face and heard himself cry out. 'Oh God, no.'

She heard him, she got up and turned, tearing her pyjama jacket open and exposing her breasts. He saw her painted nails tear into the flesh. 'Like that, Joshua. I'll torture myself if you go with my mother. I'll wound my sex, I promise you, like that, like that.'

Simon watched as she dragged her nails down over her pale breasts and saw the streaks of blood form. 'No, Caroline,' he shouted. 'Stop it.' He flung himself onto her and pinioned her arms down. But she began to struggle and bite him. They fell to the floor. Suddenly she was quiet. He got up and stepped away from her.

Her head still moved from side to side, and then her hands moved over her loins, caressing them sensually. Then she opened her eyes and stared up at Simon.

'Caroline,' he murmured helplessly.

'My mother,' she said, 'had a grey Persian cat. She doted on the cat, she fondled it more than me. One morning I took the cat into the stables. I made a noose and I hung the cat from a beam. It swung there, spitting and screaming, clawing the empty air. It jerked, twisted, and then was still. I untied it and put the corpse back on my mother's bed.'

Simon fell to his knees beside her. 'Caroline, this is all nonsense. Now, you must calm down. You know me, I'm Simon. I love you, my darling. I promised in Morocco that whatever happened, I would take care of you. Do you remember?'

She sat up on the floor and hugged her knees. 'People who

care for me only want one thing. My money. Did you hear, whatsyourname?' She got up and extended her arms. 'I'm free, because I'm rich. I'm as free as a great white bird.' She paused. 'Oh yes, I saw that bird. That was the ghost of myself. It's flown away you know.' Caroline turned and stared at Simon. Her manner abruptly changed again.

'If you don't like it here, get out of my cabin,' Caroline screamed at him. 'Remember this is my cabin and I paid for it. The cabin you booked is next door. Now get out.' Her voice was screeching with hysteria.

'Then you know I'm Simon. You recognize me?' he asked.

'Get out, get out. I don't care who you are.' She stamped her foot and pushed him towards the door.

He must go, he thought. If he went she might calm down. In the morning she might be different. The attack would be over. Christ, it must be over. What had he done? Betty had been telling him the truth that morning and he had refused to believe it. But how could someone change so completely?

Simon left the cabin. He tried the door of his own cabin. It was locked.

Caroline appeared. She was still wearing her pyjamas but she had wound a white turban round her head. 'You'd better ask the steward for the key,' she said and moved away along the alleyway.

'Where are you going?' Simon called after her.

'On deck,' she cried out. 'You can't tell me what to do any more. I'm free and I'm rich. Leave me alone. Leave me alone, I tell you.'

She moved further down the alley-way. Simon followed her. He caught up with her on the deck close to the wheelhouse. He siezed hold of her arms. With a violent twist she broke free from him. She clutched hold of a stanchion. Suddenly she leaped on to the ship's rail.

'I can fly like my ghost,' she called out.

Simon forced his voice to sound calm. 'There are sharks in the sea below you,' he said. Then he walked slowly towards her.

Caroline laughed. 'Sharks? Oh, don't be absurd. Have you

forgotten? I'm a cannibal too. Besides, I can fly. Haven't you seen me fly? You must watch.'

As she spoke, her grasp seemed to slacken on the stanchion, and Simon thought she would fall overboard.

'Caroline,' he said quietly, moving gradually towards her. 'Please don't let go. I promised I would look after you and I will. Remember that we've been happy together.'

The words now slid out of his mouth. He was hardly aware of what he was saying. 'Caroline, I love you,' he heard himself say. 'We'll forget what happened. Of course we will. Please, Caroline.'

'You don't mean what you say,' Caroline answered. 'When you came to our villa, you came as a crook. You'll always be a crook, and there is nothing that can change you. You only want my money and now you won't get a cent or a dollar of it. Besides, you're no good in bed, you're a flop. Hasn't anyone said that to you before? It's the truth,' she screamed.

Her hair was blowing away from her head. He could see her face twisted into a mask by the tortured emotions she was possessed by.

He took a step forward. He put out his arms. 'Caroline,' he whispered, 'come down, lean towards me, I'll take you to bed. You need rest, sleep, in the morning it will be different.'

'There's no morning,' she screamed at him. 'Where I live it's always night. Night. Where the ghosts of dead white birds fly.'

Simon lunged forward and as he did so Caroline jumped. She seemed to leap upwards and out, her arms high above her. He rushed to the rail. He could see her white clothes in the dark, smooth waves.

'Oh my God.' For a moment he stood there, then he turned and ran to the wheelhouse. 'She's fallen overboard,' he blurted out.

For a moment he thought of diving down to try and save her, but with every instant that passed the shape of white in the black waves was growing fainter.

But he was completely confused. He turned in a circle aimlessly as the ship erupted into activity. For the last few hours he had lived with a monster. He recalled Betty's words. 'She will take you into hell.'

It seemed a long time before the life-buoys were thrown overboard and search-lights were turned on. A sliver of white could be seen in the darkness of the ship's wake. As a lifeboat was lowered the fin of a shark appeared. The ship turned slowly.

Simon clung to the rail, his body trembling. A steward brought him a brandy. He stared down at the liquid and bemusedly wondered how he would pay for it.

On the way back, the place where she had jumped overboard $1\frac{1}{2}$ miles away could be found by the life-buoys floating in the calm sea. The water showed no trace of blood. The stained turban was drifting slowly away from the ship.